THE SUICIDE KILLER

KILLERS AMONG BOOK TWO

S. E. GREEN

PRAISE FOR THE SERIES

"The ending literally left me with my mouth hanging open–not only was it shocking, it was more than a little gruesome and bloody. In a word, perfect." ~Crimespree Magazine

"Dark and disturbing–a high stakes thriller that offers a window into a terrifying world." ~Kami Garcia, #1 NYT Bestselling Author

"S. E. Green spares no one--unique, beautifully twisted, and rich in mystery." ~Jennifer L. Armentrout, #1 NYT Bestselling Author

"A zippy, gripping psychological drama." ~Kirkus Reviews

"With an engaging and complex main character and a plot twist you'll never see, Green's thrillers are to die for." ~RT Reviews

"Readers will be most fascinated by Lane herself, an

emotion-less machine whose small twinklings of humanity are awakened as the killer gets ever closer." ~Booklist

"Readers who relish a darkly twisted crime drama with a well-managed surprise ending will enjoy curling up with this one." ~BCCB

AUTHOR'S NOTE

Everyone has a dark side, and I certainly explore mine when I write Lane.

She is the 18-year-old daughter of the infamous serial killer, The Decapitator. Lane was first introduced in *Killer Instinct* as a conflicted 16-year-old with a dark side she couldn't explain.

Now she can explain it.

Now she knows what to do with it...

I love to hear from my readers! Don't hesitate to shoot me an email shannon@segreen.net. I try my very best to respond to every message. You can also sign up for my (non-annoying) newsletter at www.segreen.net to gain access to free books and inside information.

Lane, the college student.

Lane, the dorm girl.

Lane, ready to off my roommate.

"Bye!" Sabrina, my roommate, chirps with an exuberant wave. She swings her book bag over her shoulder, double checks her lip gloss, finger combs her straight black hair and bangs out the door.

With a groan, I drop my head to my desk. One semester. I only have to make it one semester and then I can get my own apartment. Because my sister, Daisy, was right—all incoming freshmen are required to stay one semester in the dorms.

Now, though, I'm going to sleep. Between Sabrina's daytime chattiness and her nighttime snoring, I can't recall the last time I had several hours of uninterrupted sleep. It's pretty non-stop with this girl.

With a yawn, I climb up the short ladder to the top bunk, grab my down pillow, and cram it under my head. I'm halfway into a solid cycle of REM when the door bangs back open.

"Guess what?" Sabrina tosses her book bag onto the bottom bunk. "My class got canceled!"

I don't open my eyes. Maybe she'll get the hint and shut the hell up.

She whirls away and over to the mini-fridge. "Want a soda?"

I don't answer.

There's a pop, a fizz, and then a couple of gulps.

"You don't mind if I turn on music, do you?" she asks.

Oh my God, this isn't real. There is no way this girl is my roommate.

I know it's coming, but still when she turns on the opera, I groan. Leave it to me to be the only student who gets an opera lover as a roommate.

She takes one step up the ladder, and I do open my eyes now. Her head peeks up and over my mattress and when her black eyes meet mine, she grins. "I knew you weren't sleeping!"

And apparently, I won't be any time soon.

2

At home, it's no better.

Upstairs Victor, my stepdad, and Justin, my middle-school-aged brother, are yelling. Or rather Justin is the one yelling. "God, Dad, what's the big deal?"

"The big deal is that it's a school night," Victor calmly responds. "You can stay with your friend on a weekend, not a weekday. You know the rules."

"You look like shit," Daisy says, and slowly, I blink my heavy eyelids.

With a yawn, I scoot over to the couch and fall down beside her. She's got a MacBook propped open on her lap, and she turns it slightly, so I can't see what's on the screen. Interesting. She smiles a little, but it's there in her blue eyes. She's hiding something.

Closing my eyes, I lean my head back on the cushion, pretending I don't notice. "What's up with Dad and Justin?"

"It's been like this a week," she says. "They are arguing over everything. It's driving me nuts."

Upstairs Justin stomps across the hall, a door bangs

closed, and it echoes through the house. Justin's always been a low key kind of kid. I suppose he was due for this phase.

"Poor Dad," Daisy mumbles. "Tell me I was never like that."

"Not with Dad, no, but with Mom..." Opening my eyes, I roll my head to the side to look at Daisy's pretty profile. As I do, she closes the MacBook and lays it on the cushion beside her left thigh.

"Speaking of, you doing okay?" I ask.

Daisy's lips firm. "I don't want to talk about that bitch."

"Fair enough." This past summer (and unbeknownst to me) Daisy did one of those genetic tests and discovered yet another secret I've been keeping from her. She found out Victor isn't her real dad. She found out my dad is her real dad.

Yet one more thing Mom lied about.

She's digging more into Mom. Daisy wants answers, and I get it. She already knows our "perfect" mother wasn't so perfect after all, and she suspects there's more.

Part of me wants her to find out the whole truth so I have someone to share it with. But the other part, the big sister part, wants to protect her from our dark heritage.

All I can do is keep an eye on Daisy, and maybe do a little digging into her MacBook when I get a chance. Now, though, I glance over my shoulder toward the stairs that lead up to the bedrooms to make sure Victor hasn't come down. I turn back to Daisy. "You haven't told—"

"Absolutely not." She shakes her head. "It would kill him."

We both hear Victor coming down the stairs and turn to see him step into the great room. He takes one look at me, and I can tell Justin's temper tantrum has worn him out, but Victor still offers me a sweet and loving smile.

"Let me guess," he says. "Opera? Snoring? Motor-mouth?"

I laugh. "All of the above."

"You need to have a talk with her. There's only so long a person can function without sleep."

"I will." Standing up, I turn a circle, looking for my Jeep keys. "I have to get to my Patch and Paw shift."

Daisy nods to my right hand. "You're holding them."

I look down at the keys in my hand. "Oh."

"Lane," Victor sighs. "You need sleep."

Lane, the college student. Lane, the dorm girl. Lane, the sister. Lane, the daughter.

Lane, the sleep-deprived zombie.

3

At Patch and Paw, the veterinarian clinic where I have worked for years, one of the volunteers throws a handful of balls up into the air. The under-twenty-pound dogs take off in all directions, zipping and zinging across the play area.

"Is this the life or what?" the elderly volunteer asks.

I don't bother opening my eyes and instead stay leaning up against the side of the clinic. Can a person sleep standing up?

Over to my right, the side door opens and footsteps tread across the fake green turf. I recognize those steps. Dr. O'Neal always digs her right heel in when she walks.

"Lane," she says.

"Hm?"

"Lane!"

I open one eye to see Dr. O'Neal staring at me in stark contrast to her usual gleeful and way-too-happy personality. She folds her arms, and I open both eyes. I'm not usually nervous around Dr. O'Neal, but right now she's alarming me. I've never seen her glare.

She says, "When you asked me if you could stay on and train under me as you went through your undergrad in Biology, I was very excited. But I have to tell you, ever since you started college, you've been a real disappointment around here."

I push off the wall, fully awake now. "What happened?"

"The question is more, what hasn't happened? You were supposed to draw blood on the Rottweiler. Place a catheter in the mixed breed lab. Give medication to the elderly cat that was brought in this morning. And thirty minutes ago you were supposed to assist me with surgery."

That can't be right. I search my brain... "I thought that was my list for tomorrow."

"You wanted more responsibility around here, and I gave it to you. But so far you're not proving you can handle it."

"I can." I straighten up. "I haven't been getting enough sleep."

Dr. O'Neal is a petite woman, but right now she's not so small as she continues glaring at me. "I'm a single mom with two kids under the age of five. I don't get a whole lot of sleep either. But you don't see me walking around here yawning, bleary-eyed, forgetting my work, and falling asleep on the job."

Oh, shit, I'm totally getting schooled by this woman. I nod. "You're right. I apologize. You can count on me. I promise."

She doesn't respond to that and instead just stares up into my eyes, and while she does, I try to show her how really sorry I am. Whatever she sees must appease her because she nods, spins on her heel, and disappears back through the side door.

"Phew," the elderly volunteer says. "I have never seen her angry. You okay?"

With a nod, I head inside too.

As is usual when it comes to Dr. O'Neal, I compare her to my former boss, Dr. Issa, whom I had a thing for and whom I greatly admired. The truth is, he would have handled the situation exactly the same. And for that, Dr. O'Neal officially just earned my respect.

Frankly, I'm lucky she didn't fire me.

fter my shift at Patch and Paw, I swing by Judge Penn's court. It's on my way back to campus and so I might as well. Plus, I haven't been by since Adam left, and Penn's court is my happy place.

Adam, Judge Penn's nephew, and I had quite the roller coaster friendship to include each of us sharing the other's vigilante ways. It was touch and go for a while, and at one point we even tried to frame the other.

Now, though, we're at a good spot. Adam is overseas in an exchange program, and we share periodic texts. His dog, Sally, is doing well. Surprisingly, Adam's mom fell in love with her and decided to keep her.

It's the end of the day, and Penn's likely closing down whatever case he's hearing. Still, though, I go because I need a happy place right now.

Penn sees me push through the back doors and gives me a slight nod of acknowledgment. I've been here a lot over the years, and he's used to seeing me. But now he also knows me as Adam's friend.

As I slide into my usual spot along the back, his gavel

comes down and an entire row of people sitting in front sob. A mousy-haired woman who I'd place in her forties shuffles from the defendant's table and down the aisle. She's wearing a dress two sizes too big, clunky black heels, and a black velvet headband holding back her stringy hair.

I don't know who dressed her, but the whole thing is just wrong.

She keeps her head down, not making eye contact.

A gray-haired man from the row of sobbing people shoots to his feet. He points a finger at the woman. "You'll pay for what you did to my grandson. Do you hear me? You will pay!"

The woman continues to keep her head ducked low. I expect Penn to hit his gavel and tell the room to quiet down, but he doesn't. He simply watches her go, his face set into a hard line. He knows she's guilty.

If Penn knows it, then it's true. If there's one thing I've learned about him over the years, it's just that. He knows when someone is getting away with their evil deed.

What evil deed, though?

Eventually, the room empties out, and I head straight into the hall where the docket for the day is listed on the wall. It's the last case of the day, and I read the defendant's name.

Rachelle Gentry.

Well, hello, Rachelle Gentry. Let's see who you are.

"This is an injustice!" the gray-haired man says into the mic. "My grandson was molested by this woman. And, what, because he was drugged and can't remember the specifics, because there's no hard evidence, this woman, Rachelle Gentry, goes free? She stole his innocence and no one cares. No one!"

Outside the courthouse, I shift to tuck in behind a column and listen.

"He's twelve goddamn years old," the gray-haired man says. "Someone needs to care!"

I care.

He ticks off his fingers as reporters listen closely. "Rachelle Gentry is a convicted pedophile. She did five years for having an ongoing sexual relationship with one of her students. He was only thirteen! How is it, I ask, that this woman was hired to be a tutor upon being released from prison? How is it this woman was left in a room alone with my grandson? How is it she was allowed to leave campus with him and go to a motel? Who the hell dropped the ball on doing a background check?"

The gray-haired man bangs his fist on the podium. "I want her to suffer in the worst way. She took his innocence, and he will never be the same. Never! You think she's going to stop? Rachelle Gentry is a registered sex offender and she will do this again. Mark my words, she will."

Reporters yell questions at him, and the gray-haired man wraps his arm around a younger woman, probably his daughter, and the two of them walk down the courthouse steps.

Biker Dudes Against Pedophiles—BDAP—pops into my mind. My intentions with Mr. Oily Nose, the pedophile I found lurking months ago around Justin, was to deliver him to BDAP, but, of course, I dealt with him in my own way.

This Rachelle Gentry, though. I do believe she's a perfect candidate for BDAP. She thinks she's skirted her way out of this one, but she should be worried. Very worried.

Life's been busy. I haven't had a chance to exercise that certain other part of me. That part that loves to deliver justice when the law fails. Yes, it's beyond time to touch base with my extracurricular side. I'll rough Rachelle up, this time not going as far as I did with Mr. Oily Nose, and then deliver her to BDAP.

Yes, perfect.

"We got a body," one cop says to another as they pass by me going down the courthouse steps. "A woman in her twenties. I hear there's a lot of blood."

"Suicide?" the other one asks.

"Not sure, but I did hear one of the detectives say there's some questionable evidence."

Stepping away from my spot tucked behind the column, I head down the courthouse steps, too. I need something new, and sometimes it just falls into your lap. Like this

Rachelle Gentry woman, and now this questionable-evidence suicide.

I f I could live in my Jeep, I would. It's peaceful. It's quiet. It's all mine.

No snoring roommate. No list of things to do at Patch and Paw. No angsty brother fighting with Victor.

Just me, my iPad, homework, this tree I'm currently parked under, the brisk evening breeze blowing through my open windows, and thoughts of Rachelle Gentry.

I love the internet. It's the greatest invention ever, and nowadays you don't need to be Reggie, my techy best friend at MIT, to find something out.

Like the fact Rachelle lives thirty miles away in a mobile home park far from children. When you're a registered sex offender, there's only so many places you can live, and lucky for me, the mobile home park sits in the woods of Woodbridge and is fairly deserted.

According to my search, there are twenty lots and only six have mobile homes on them. This will be perfect. I'll do a little recon, get some homework done, and then I'll sleep. I'll go to my boyfriend Tommy's place for that.

Boyfriend. It's odd thinking that word. Who would've thought, me, dark-side Lane, would have a boyfriend?

Tommy's working late stocking shelves at Whole Foods. I'll shoot him a quick text. I'll let myself in with his hide-a-key and crash. He won't mind.

But first Rachelle. At this time of day, it might take me forty-five minutes to get there.

As I put my iPad aside and crank my engine, my phone rings. It's Daisy. "Hello?" I say.

She sighs. "Will you please talk to Justin?"

"What's going on?"

"Dad's working late and I'm watching Justin, but he's being a real butthole."

"I heard that!" Justin yells.

Daisy lowers her voice. "I'm totally ready to let him rule this house just to shut him up."

"You know that's not how it works. Put him on."

There's a little back and forth between them and finally Justin's voice. "What?" he snips.

Taking a breath, I remind myself I love my little brother. "What's the problem?"

"Daisy won't let me stay up and watch *It*. God, I can't wait to be like you so I can do what I want."

Believe me, kid, it doesn't work that way. "Justin, you are in middle school. Your bedtime is nine p.m. That was my bedtime at your age, and that was Daisy's bedtime at your age. Just because you're the youngest doesn't mean you get special treatment. You have to follow the same rules. Plus, *It* is not an appropriate movie for you to be watching. Now, why don't you tell me the real reason you've been a pain lately. Because, Justin, this isn't you. You are a sweet, caring, and funny boy. You're not this mean and irritable kid you've been showing around the house. Is there something going on at school?"

A long stretch of silence follows, and I wait. I'm good at waiting.

Finally, he sighs. "It's nothing. I'm fine. I'll listen to Daisy. Bye." He hangs up, and I make a mental note to check in with some of his friends because there's something going on, possibly at school.

7

It's nine at night by the time I arrive at Rachelle Gentry's run-down mobile home. Tonight's about a little surveillance, then I'll finish up homework, get some sleep at Tommy's, wake up and go to my morning classes, do my Patch and Paw shift, go home and search Daisy's MacBook, and at some point, I need to dig into Justin.

This isn't how I envisioned my life, but I can deal. It is what it is. A logical side of me says to eliminate stuff from my list. I can't eliminate family, or school, or work, which leaves my extracurricular activities.

But those, those are what drive me. Like right now Rachelle Gentry is in there deep, nibbling away, reminding me how much I love—no, how much I *need* this.

With my lights off and my Jeep lurking in the shadows, I survey the deserted mobile home park. Of the six trailers here and propped up on blocks, I wonder how many contain deviants just like Rachelle Gentry, the pedophile.

There are no security cameras, and only one lone yellow street light flicks in the darkness. The trailers sit spaced far enough away that no one cares about their neighbor. Six trailers in all, three with lights on inside, and the one farthest away with its lopsided porch and patchwork roof belongs to Rachelle Gentry.

I'm liking this broken down place. It's fitting for what I have in mind.

Where did she live before her prison stint for that thirteen-year-old kid? She's a former social worker. She probably had a decent apartment somewhere. But then she gave in to her urges and this is her life now.

It's a far cry from what she really deserves, and soon the BDAP will show her just that. I can't wait to deliver her all wrapped up neat and tidy with the evidence I'll compile and, of course, a bit of my own brand of justice, too. Between me and the BDAP, she'll be worked over nicely.

I close my eyes, fantasizing a bit about things to come. The perfect sister, daughter, and girlfriend would be elsewhere right now, but no one, especially not me, claims I'm perfect.

A knocking on my window has me shooting straight up in my seat to see Rachelle Gentry looking right at me.

Shit.

Shit. Shit. Shit.

With a little smile, I roll my window down. "Yes?"

She doesn't smile back. "I'm part of the neighborhood watch. What are you doing parked here?"

Neighborhood watch? She's got to be kidding. There's nothing around. "Actually I was tired and pulled over to grab a few minutes of sleep." It's not a bad response and partly true.

She runs her fingers through her limp mousy hair before folding her arms to survey me. Back in the courtroom, she had on a suit two sizes too big. But now standing here in front of me, I get it.

In her tight long sleeve top, cut off jean shorts, and thigh-high boots, she's rocking a body any horny kid would want to be in, out, and all over. Well, that and the fact she puts out is the big lure for boys of all ages.

I have no clue if she remembers me from the courtroom. Maybe she thinks I'm a reporter or something. Either way, she now knows what I look like. And she's got more of an attitude than I initially thought because back in Penn's courtroom, she was all timid and meek.

I crank my engine. "I'll go home and get some sleep. Sorry about this."

In response, she hikes her chin, like she's throwing me an extra threat.

Please, I'll extra threat her.

Bottom line, her home is now officially off limits. Which means I have to grab her somewhere else. It's a higher degree of difficulty, but I don't have a choice. If I want to be around for my family, I have to be careful with my steps.

As I pull away, I eye her in the rearview as she walks back to her mobile home. I would love to savor the justice this woman deserves. But this life of mine is now about sacrifice.

Can I do this? Can I really have it all? Sister, daughter, girlfriend, student, killer.

Killer.

It's taken me a while to wrap my brain around that word, killer, and to admit it to myself. But it's who I am, though it's only a part. My family always comes first. I never want to get another call like when my stepdad had a heart attack and was in the ER. I was indulging in a bit of vigilante justice and had my phone off.

It was one of the worst nights of my life, and I never want to experience that again.

Yes, my family will always come first. Perhaps it's more about reorganizing the way I do things, all while satisfying the darkness in me that I can't ignore.

I find Tommy's hide-a-key right where he said it would be—hidden in a piece of fake dog poop. Cute, Tommy, cute.

Dropping my stuff in his living room, I drag myself into his bathroom and as I brush my teeth, I look at myself in the medicine cabinet mirror. Boy, I look rough.

My red curly hair is in dire need of cleaning and dark shadows dig deep into the skin below my green eyes. Hell, even my freckles look tired.

I really want to go straight to bed, but I also need a shower. Flicking on the spray, I turn it lukewarm and step inside. I hate hot showers. My core temp already runs hot and heated water only makes it worse.

I stand with my eyes closed, letting the water run down my body. I need to shave my legs but clean hair is more important. I'll shave tomorrow.

Grabbing Tommy's tee-tree shampoo, I lather up my head and while it tingles my scalp I work on my body next. I'm in the middle of rinsing when the bathroom door opens and Tommy steps inside.

I look at him through the glass door, all six feet of lean muscle, and his short blond hair mussed from his motorcycle helmet. Standing fully dressed in jeans and a snug tee, he folds his arms and casually leans back against the door as he slowly takes me in.

I'm not so tired now.

"So," he says. "You're naked."

Tipping my head back, I let the water stream across my scalp and down my body, becoming hyper-aware of it trailing over my skin. "Yes, I am."

"But you're here to sleep," he says.

Turning the faucet off, I squeeze the water from my hair and slide open the glass door. I take a towel, and as I keep my eyes fastened to his blue ones, I slowly dry off.

"Orgasms make a person sleep better." I step out of the shower and onto the rug. Bending over, I wrap the towel around my shoulder length wet hair and stand back up.

Tommy's eyes go straight to my breasts. "I'm glad I found someone to cover the rest of my shift. I was kind of hoping to talk you into a little naughty, horny, mutual gratification."

Pushing off the door, he steps forward and trails his index finger from my throat, down between my breasts, over my stomach, and at the last second, turns his hand to get a better angle as he goes lower still.

My eyes close on a breath. What's interesting about me and Tommy is that we've never experienced actual penetration. We've done everything else, but for some reason, he hasn't gone inside of me yet.

Hell, I gave him a blow job before we actually even kissed. So, yeah, the sexual part of our relationship is interesting. But we just roll with it. What happens, happens, and we're both cool with that.

Fixing me with a hungry look, he lowers his voice. "Let's take care of you and then tomorrow after you sleep, we'll worry about me."

The next afternoon at Patch and Paw, I double check I've done all of my duties, and I take Corn Chip out into the side yard to play.

For as long as I've worked here, Corn Chip has been around. He's a mixed-breed, medium-sized dog with gray scraggly hair and white eyebrows, and he's my best friend. His mom travels a lot with work and so she boards him here on a regular basis.

I tell him things I don't tell anybody else. Like now as I say, "Want to know a secret? I'm going to turn Rachelle Gentry over to Biker Dudes against Pedophiles. And I'm going to be in control this time. Last time I got a little side-tracked with Mr. Oily Nose."

Corn Chip's white eyebrows twitch and I rub the tip of his ear. "Remember him? I gouged his eyes out for looking at child porn." The memory makes me sigh, and Corn Chip leans into my hand to get a better rub.

"You're such a good boy," I say, and his tail wags. We play a little tug-of-war with a braided rope, and when he playfully growls, I chuckle. "So mean, you."

"You're very good with him," Dr. O'Neal says, and I go still.

This exact thing happened with Dr. Issa. He overheard me telling Corn Chip my secrets. I ended up kissing him to distract him, but I can't very well kiss Dr. O'Neal.

Or maybe I can.

I eye her lips, but I have no clue how much, if any, of that she just heard and so I wait to see.

She steps around where I sit on the green turf and lowers herself down across from me. As she runs her hand down Corn Chip's back, she looks at me. "I owe you an apology. I didn't handle things with you very well last time."

"You don't need to apologize. You're the boss, and I deserved to be reprimanded."

Dr. O'Neal just looks at me. "You know, when I first met you I thought you were a bit, well, odd."

I nod. "I get that. I found you to be annoyingly perky."

She laughs. "And I get that. But now I really like you, Lane."

"I like you, too," I respond, surprised to find I mean it. Who would've thought me and Dr. O'Neal friends? Not I.

10

After my Patch and Paw shift, I head home with full intentions of snooping in Daisy's room. This is her volunteer night at the library where she tutors middle school kids and she usually doesn't get home until 8.

No one is home and I head straight up the stairs and into her room. I find her MacBook wedged under her pillow, and sitting down on her bed, I open the lid. As expected it's password protected, but she uses the same password for everything and so I quickly type it in.

An audio file sits open on her screen and I read the description: *Phone call with Mom's high school boyfriend.*

Wow, look at Daisy tracking down stuff I've never even thought of.

I press play.

Daisy: Hi, I'm Daisy and I'm the daughter of Suzie Cameron.

Old boyfriend: *silence*. Wow, that's a name I haven't heard in a while.

Daisy: I'm not sure if you know, but she passed away.

Old boyfriend: No... I hadn't heard. I'm so sorry.

Daisy: Thank you.

Old boyfriend: How can I help you?

Daisy: I'm putting together memory books for my sister and brother and was hoping you'd tell me what she was like in high school.

Old boyfriend: Well, she was driven. Focused. She always got what she wanted.

Daisy: Is that how she got you?

Old boyfriend: *laughter*. I wish. I was more of a prop on her arm. Something she thought she needed.

Daisy: You mean like to look normal?

Old boyfriend: Huh, never thought of it that way, but yeah. Probably.

Daisy: I'm sorry for the question I'm about to ask, but did she ever cheat on you?

Old boyfriend: This is about more than memory books, isn't it?

Daisy: Yes, but I hope you'll still talk to me.

Old boyfriend: Cheating... I never actually caught her, but I sensed there was someone or something else that occupied her time.

Daisy: What do you mean *something* else?

Old boyfriend: Not sure. Again, just a feeling I always had.

Daisy: Anything else you can tell me?

Old boyfriend: Just that she was a great girl. We dated about a year and we always had fun. Your mom was adventurous. She was a true gift to this world. You should focus on that and not anything else.

Daisy: Great, thank you for your time.

Old boyfriend: Oh, wait a minute. Whatever happened to her older sister?

Daisy: *silence*. She had a *sister*?

Old boyfriend: Yeah, her name was Marji. She was a weird one, but Suzie sure liked her, so I rolled with it. The three of us hung out quite often.

Daisy: To be honest with you, I didn't know my mom had a sister. Thank you for the information.

They end the call, and all I can think is, *Shit, she knows about Aunt Marji.*

Aunt Marji, another demented relative.

Aunt Marji, who made me harm animals.

Aunt Marji, who kidnapped and tortured people.

Aunt Marji, my first pre-meditated kill.

11

D ownstairs Victor's on the phone. I didn't realize he'd come home. Whoever he's talking to is on speaker.

A man says, "Yesterday there was a body found in Alexandria—woman, early twenties, who had sliced into her own neck. The poor son woke up from a nap and found her. Apparent suicide."

Woman in her twenties, a lot of blood, suicide. This must be what I overheard those two cops talking about at the courthouse.

Victor says, "Not to be rude, but what does this have to do with me?"

The man clears his throat. "We've now had a chance to dissect the scene and there was some blood found that didn't belong to the victim."

The questionable evidence.

Victor says, "Okay, and?"

"It belonged to your wife."

Silence.

From my spot on the stairwell, my body sways, and I grab onto the banister to keep upright.

"The sample is degraded," the man says, "but it's a match."

Victor clears his throat. "Degraded as in...?"

"As in old. One of the tech's found it in a nearby closet. They're estimating that it's been there forty years."

More silence.

I hold my breath, waiting to hear what's said next, and as I do my heart picks up pace to the point it slashes through my body. Pressing the palm of my right hand into my chest, I make myself exhale, inhale, exhale...

Again, Victor clears his throat. "To be clear, my wife would have been five years old forty years ago."

"Yes, I know. Also, I did some digging and forty years ago the exact same suicide occurred in that house. A woman had sliced her own neck and the child was the one who found her."

More silence. "What's the address?"

The man rattles it off, and I make a mental note. Victor rushes out of the house, not even seeing me on the stairwell, and for several minutes, I don't move.

Forty years ago a woman killed herself. Fast forward and the exact same suicide occurs in the exact same house. Both women found by their children.

Why would Mom's DNA be in this place?

My phone buzzes with a text from Victor: I HAD AN EMERGENCY COME UP. CAN YOU PICK UP JUSTIN FROM AIKIDO?

For one brief second, I consider ignoring the text. I'd much rather be racing to Alexandria and the address Victor is currently headed to. But the truth is, there's nothing I can do there but hide in the shadows and watch. There's no way I'd get inside that house.

Plus, haven't I been reminding myself that family comes first?

YES, I type back.

Ten minutes later, I pull into the building where Justin and I both take Aikido lessons. Daisy did, too, for a while but eventually lost interest.

Dressed in his hakama, Justin is already outside waiting and it strikes me as odd. He normally hangs out inside after class is over.

He catches sight of my Jeep, and with a sigh, he pushes away from the brick building and trudges over. Opening the door, he takes the one step up and swings inside. Without looking at me, he shuts the door, props his elbow in the sill, and looks at the Aikido building. Through the front windows, another class has already begun.

"You all right?" I ask.

"Fine."

Tilting forward, I get a good look at his face and specifically the bruise on his chin. I've had my fair share of bruises from Aikido class and so it's not unusual to see an occasional one on Justin. Still, I ask, "You give as good as you got there?"

"Mm, hm."

I keep staring at his dark hair and the side of his face. There's no mistake he's Victor's son. Justin is most definitely a mini-Victor.

Finally, he looks over at me. "We going or what?"

I keep looking at him for another beat or two. "Yeah, we're going." I put my Jeep in gear and pull away.

A few small months ago this wouldn't have been him. We'd be talking, or rather he'd be talking about all kinds of stuff.

I drive a few blocks, my brain cycling with conversation starters. Odd, I've never struggled to talk to Justin. I glance over at him again. His hair rustles in the chilly breeze coming in the cracked window as he watches the trees, cars, and buildings go by.

"How about I come to your next class?" I suggest.

He glances over. "Why?"

"Because I want to."

"Um...I don't think so."

I downshift. "Why is that?"

He shrugs. "Because...because I said so."

With a nod, I turn on my blinker. "Okay, I respect that."

Yeah, no I don't. Something is up, and I'm going to find out what.

With Justin home from Aikido and in the shower, I'm in Victor's office using his computer. I dig around, searching for anything on the forty-year-ago suicide.

But other than the facts I already know, I get nothing.

Is it some weird kismet that the same exact suicide would occur forty years later in the exact same house? Maybe, but if there's one thing I've learned, it's to listen to my gut instinct. And my gut says something is up.

On the screen of Victor's computer is the old newspaper article from forty years ago. Gloria Michaels was the woman's name. The young daughter found her, though her name isn't listed.

I stare at the small print of the equally small article, and something niggles away at my memory—like I've seen this exact article before, though I can't quite place where.

With the degraded DNA sample of my mother, Victor's going to be interested in the house and its history. He could very well tap into the FBI's resources for this. Though that would have to be on the down low. I don't imagine the FBI will give Victor official approval for some degraded DNA.

Either way, dots are to be connected. Why would Mom's blood be in this house? How is it that two suicides occurred exactly forty years apart in the same place? Whoever is investigating this will be interested in the recent suicide and if there was foul play. That's fine because I'm more interested in Mom's blood.

Mom's past.

I never met her parents, my grandparents. They died in a car accident before I was born and when Mom was in her early twenties—at least that's what she told us. Who the hell knows if that is the truth? Because she never told us about her sister, Aunt Marji, either.

Does Victor know something I don't? Maybe. He knew about Marji. Or at least he had met her a few times and he didn't like her. Does he know Marji and Mom were sisters? I'm not sure. He's never said. When he and I spoke about Marji, he knew her as Mom's childhood friend.

He certainly doesn't know they were both serial killers.

Everything about my mom is buried deep.

Mom's past. Justin. Daisy. Rachelle Gentry. School. Work. Tommy. Victor. These are all the things that need my attention. It's a lot to juggle, but I can manage all the moving parts. I like marking things off my "To Do" list.

Rachelle Gentry will be the easiest. I'll quickly mark her off. It'll give me a sense of accomplishment.

Through the walls of Victor's office, I hear the front door open. It's a bit past eight and likely Daisy. Grabbing my notes, I shut down Victor's computer and emerge.

From the kitchen, Daisy glances over. "What are you doing here?"

"Dad had a work emergency and asked me to pick up Justin. Speaking of, do you think he's being bullied?"

My sister gives that some thought. "Maybe, it might explain his attitude. Why, what are you thinking?"

"He's got a fresh bruise on his chin, and he's sulking. It reminds me of that eighteen-year-old guy who was bullying Justin and a bunch of his friends a couple of years ago." Granted I tracked the guy down and taught him my version of a lesson, but still.

"Okay." Daisy nods. "Let's both keep an eye out."

She dishes up cold spaghetti and takes a couple of hungry bites. Her recent research into Mom's past trickles back in and I debate whether to tell her about Aunt Marji. If I do, maybe it'll show her she can share things with me, too.

With a mouth full of meat and noodles, she glances up. "What?"

She might find the timing coincidental, but I forge ahead anyway. "I want you to know that Mom had a sister. Her name was Marji. I found out about her after Mom died. She sent us a condolence card."

Daisy swallows. "What the hell? Why are you just now telling me about her?"

Because I know you know. "Because I went to see her, and she was awful. I didn't want you and Justin to ever meet her."

"Where does she live?"

"Richmond," I say. "Or at least she did. I believe she moved." Or rather was killed—by me. "I drove by her house months ago and there was a For Sale sign in her yard."

"Wow." Daisy puts the Tupperware bowl on the counter.

"Yeah." I wait, hoping she'll share and not suspect I was digging into her laptop.

She sighs. "Well, you should know I talked to Mom's

high school boyfriend. He actually mentioned Marji, so I already knew. Or actually, I just found out. I was going to tell you."

"Sure, yeah." Shifting, I prop my hip against the counter. "Did the boyfriend mention anything else?"

"Just that Mom was a great girl and that Marji was a weird one. Also, he thought Mom had something else going on."

"What do you mean?"

Daisy shakes her head. "No clue, it was just a feeling he had."

With a nod, I give the space between us time to breathe, waiting to see if there's anything else she wants to divulge. She now knows Seth, my real father, is her real father. And she now knows Mom had a secret sister, Marji.

It's a lot.

My gut tells me she's not giving up. Daisy wants more. Yet in this moment I'm not sure what else to share. I decide on Seth. With a glance over my shoulder to make sure Justin is still upstairs, I say, "Would you like to know everything I know about our real father?"

With a relieved breath, she nods.

I place my folder of printed research from Victor's computer on the counter, and I grab a fork. We both jump up on the kitchen island, and with the spaghetti between us, I twirl up a bite. "Our father died of colon cancer. He was raised by a preacher and his wife. The preacher, our grandfather, was not a nice man. He horribly abused our grandmother. She committed suicide."

Daisy doesn't even react, as if she already knows some stuff. "And our grandfather?" she asks.

"Mom told me Seth was defending our grandmother and accidentally killed our grandfather." That's partly true.

Mom told me Seth was defending his brother, our uncle and The Decapitator, but our uncle is a fictitious person the whole world thinks is a serial killer.

When in reality, The Decapitator is, of course, Mom.

My sister reaches in the Tupperware, picks out a chunk of tomato, and puts it in her mouth. "An uncle who was a serial killer. A grandfather who was abusive. And a father who killed his father defending his mother who committed suicide. That's some legacy we have."

"Hm."

"So what about Seth?"

"Mom told me they met in the Marines. She said he had a good sense of humor but was also stoic. She said he didn't want anything to do with me and signed over parental rights to Victor."

"And me?"

Like Daisy, I find a chunk of tomato and put it in my mouth. "Honestly, I'm not even sure he knew you were his. I found the DNA paperwork hidden in a lockbox. He and Mom probably fooled around behind Victor's back. She got pregnant and told Victor you were his."

Gripping the sides of the counter, Daisy looks down at the tile floor. I wait to see what she'll say, but nothing comes.

"Daisy, it's a lot. I wish I could tell you not to think about it, but it's there. When I found out, it was all I *could* think about. I didn't want you to know. I wanted to protect you. I hope you understand."

She nods. "You're being a protective big sister. I get it."

Reaching across the small space, I gently squeeze her shoulder. "Just don't shut me out. Talk to me, okay? No matter what you find, talk to me."

She glances over. "You knew I talked to Mom's old high school boyfriend, didn't you?"

If there's one thing I'm good at, it's lying, but now is not the time. "Yes, I went on your computer. I knew you were digging for information. I did, too, when I first found out."

"Is there more?" she asks.

The front door opens, and Victor walks in.

She lowers her voice. "Is there?"

I nod toward Victor, lowering my voice, too. "Yes, we'll talk later."

Victor tosses his keys onto the dining room table and crosses into the kitchen. He comes to an abrupt stop when he sees us sitting side by side on the counter sharing spaghetti.

Daisy says, "Hey, Dad."

"Hey, girls."

I study his expression, trying to get a read, but he looks normal. Not tired, worn out, confused, or anything else. Maybe he's already figured out the degraded DNA sample and there's a logical reason it was there.

But probably not.

He holds up a finger. "Lane, I got you something." He disappears into his office and comes back holding a white zipper pouch. "They're noise canceling headphones. With your loud roommate, I figured they'd help."

I love Victor. "Thanks, Dad."

"Sure thing." He places them on the counter next to the folder with the printed research. "What's this?"

"I used your computer to print off things for school," I say.

With a nod, he grabs a fork and dives into the spaghetti, too.

And together the three of us talk and share spaghetti, like we're just a normal family and not keeping secrets from each other.

14

Rachelle Gentry. It's out of my way, but I'll drive by her mobile home before going back to the dorms. At this time of night, it only takes me thirty minutes to get there. It'll take me thirty more to get back to the dorms, which is perfect because then my roommate will be fast asleep and I'll avoid all conversation with her.

Unless I can talk Tommy into another sleepover. I'm driving and so I send him a quick voice text: ANY INTEREST IN ANOTHER SLEEPOVER?

As I wait for his response, I bring up Daisy's name, surprised to find she hasn't texted me. With my parting words, I thought for sure she would. Interesting.

My phone buzzes with Tommy's response: CAN'T. BUSY TONIGHT.

OK, I voice text back. Now most girls would probably dive down a paranoid slope of *Is he cheating on me? Why is he busy? Why doesn't he want to see me?* Luckily, my mind doesn't do those things. I am honestly cool with him doing his thing, me doing my thing, and us doing stuff together.

It's all good.

Rachelle Gentry is on my list of things to do. I was going to wait, figure out her patterns, plot, plan, then deliver her to the BDAP. But with the repeat suicides and Mom's degraded DNA, I'm now more in the mood to get her off of my "List of things to do".

Tonight is not the night, but I do want to do another drive by. And in an intriguing way, I'm now thinking that I *want* her to see me again. I want her to *feel* as if something is coming. Perhaps it's because of her cocky attitude with me when she and I met.

As I slow to make the turn onto her road, a rumbling fills the air. It reminds of that time my family did a road trip to Florida which just happened to coincide with bike week.

Bike week.

Biker Dudes against Pedophiles.

BDAP.

Holy crap, they're here.

I pull my Jeep off the side of the road and kill my lights, more excited than I've been in quite a while. The rumbling gets close, coming down the road I was about to turn on. I slide down in my seat as first one bike goes by, then another, and another—all dressed in black with shaded helmets. Not one of them glances my way.

A motorcycle in the middle of the pack has a small enclosed trailer attached with Rachelle Gentry likely inside. Delight tickles through my blood, and I scoot up a little in my seat. I'd give anything to follow. What fun they're going to have tonight.

They continue to pass me, roughly twenty in all, and one of the bikes at the end catches my eyes. Black and silver with red fenders. I've been on that bike. Through his shaded helmet, the rider glances over at my Jeep, and I don't duck out of sight, I boldly look back.

Our gazes catch and hold, and then he's gone with his pack.

Tommy.

I knew he was hiding something.

The rumbling gradually fades as they disappear down the dark road. I turn the key in my Jeep and pull out, and my lips curve into a smile the entire way back to the dorm. If I thought Tommy was hot before, he's beyond hot now.

I saw him. He knows I saw him. And he won't hide it. He'll bring it up. He knows I'll bring it up, too. It'll be an interesting conversation. He'll want to know why I was there. I'll have to come up with a plausible reason because Woodbridge is not near my home or my dorm.

Perhaps I'll tell him the truth. I'll have to think about it.

Some thirty minutes later, I park in my dorm's lot and make my way inside. It's close to midnight now, and my roommate, Sabrina, is—as expected—fast asleep. I strip down and slide into a sleeping tee, and with the noise cancellation headphones, I climb up onto the top bunk.

I plug the headphones into a rain app, and as the pattering noise fills my ears, I settle into my down pillow. Sleep pulls at me, and right as I begin that lovely slide into it, Sabrina's snore rips through the room.

My eyes fly open.

You've got to be kidding me.

15

The college experience. It's a ritual that most kids do because they're supposed to. Half probably have no clue what they're "going to be" when they grow up. The majority are just excited to be away from home. Some will go through all four years, changing majors. Others will graduate and roll right into a Masters because there are no jobs and what else are they going to do?

And then there are those like me—get in, get out. I know why I'm here, exactly what classes I need, and I also am one hundred percent sure what I want to be—a veterinarian. I've always wanted to be a vet because animals, well, they're just awesome.

It's the people in the world that tend to suck.

"Want a chocolate covered espresso bean?" Sabrina asks as we weave our way across the common area, heading to our morning classes.

I glance down at the bag she's holding out. "Actually, yeah." I take a few and toss them all into my mouth.

"Whoa, easy." She laughs.

I ignore her as I crunch. "Listen, we've got to talk."

With a grin, she waves at a petite girl standing all the way across the lawn. "She's in my Lit class."

"You snore." I like to get right to the point. "Are you aware of this?"

Sabrina cringes. "Yes, I'm *so* sorry. I've tried all of the over the counter stuff and nothing works."

I roll a bean around in my mouth, crunching and swallowing. "So here's the thing. We've got to figure it out. Because we're roommates, we're stuck with each other, and I need sleep."

She steps around a group of guys huddled and talking before glancing back over at me. "Is it really that bad?"

I stop walking. "Last night I had noise cancellation headphones on, a rain app, and a pillow over my head. Yeah, it's an issue."

"And here I thought my opera music would be your biggest complaint," she jokes.

Picking battles is important, and snoring wins out over opera. "Why don't you do a sleep study? This is a campus. Surely they do those here somewhere. Go volunteer and see what's up. Maybe get one of those face masks people wear."

Sabrina folds the espresso bag over and tucks it down inside her book bag. "Okay, I'll figure it out."

See, a little communication can go a long way.

From the front mesh pocket of her backpack, her phone plays *All About That Bass.* She ignores it. "It's my annoying brother. I'm not getting it."

"Lane?" I glance over my shoulder. A dark-haired guy weaves his way through clumps of students as he heads toward me.

I blink. "Zach?"

With a laugh, he closes the last few feet between us and

he wraps me up in a warm hug. Boy-scented body wash. It's what he always smelled liked and he still does.

Still laughing, he steps out of the hug and his brown eyes touch on my hair and face. "You look exactly the same, well, except for the shorter hair."

Smiling, I take in his wavy dark hair, longer than it was before and a scruffy short beard. When we dated, or hung out, or had sex—whatever you want to call it—he was always cleanly shaven. "What are you doing here?"

"I'm dual enrolled. I only had one class left to graduate high school and I'm doing that one online. I also snagged a partial baseball scholarship." He grins. "I thought you were going to UVA."

"I wanted to stay close for my family." The last I saw Zach was at his brother's, Dr. Issa's, funeral. Zach and his dad moved out of state and we haven't talked since. "How long you been back?"

"A few weeks now." He cringes. "Sorry I didn't call."

"All good."

Behind me, Sabrina clears her throat, and I roll my eyes, which makes Zach laugh some more. God, I'd forgotten how much he smiles and laughs.

Stepping to the side, I make the introductions. "Sabrina, my roommate, meet Zach, a friend from high school."

"Actually we used to date," Zach corrects me as he shakes Sabrina's hand.

Sabrina's dark eyes light up with curiosity. "Ooh, really. And no bad blood?"

Well, let's see. My mother, The Decapitator, kidnapped Zach and had him unconscious in the kill room and ready to be butchered. Then my copycat, Catalina, killed Zach's brother, Dr. Issa, and left his body in a deserted building. Of course, Zach doesn't know my connection to either event, but still.

"Of course not," Zach answers Sabrina's question. He looks back at me. "Is your number still the same? I have to get to class but would love to catch up."

"Sure, sounds good."

With a big grin and a wave, he jogs off.

Sabrina's eyes pop wide. "Um, hello. Can anyone say cute?"

Yes, he is that.

Her phone rings again, this time with *The Final Countdown.* "That would be my aunt. I'm not getting that one either."

If two people from her family have called her that close together, it could be important. But it's her life, not mine. "Listen, I've got to get to class, too," I say.

"Right-o." With a salute, she heads off toward her class, and I turn to cut across the parking lot toward my building on the other side of campus.

I check my phone to see if Tommy's texted, but nothing. That's okay. I'll wait for him to come to me.

A quick stop at my Jeep, I grab a book from the back and high-tail it to class. I only have two sessions this morning and then I'm free. I'm caught up on reading and homework, and this is my day off from Patch and Paw. Daisy and Justin are both in school. I fully intend on spending my free time diving into the degraded DNA.

But a couple of hours later I climb into my Jeep, crank the engine, it turns over exactly once, and then dies.

Of course.

16

"I'll take you everywhere you need to go!" Sabrina announces.

Inwardly I groan. This can't be happening.

I toss my phone down on my bed, having just hung up from a series of calls to a mechanic, a tow truck service, and back to the mechanic. It's not looking good.

She grins. "That's what roomies are for, right?"

"Right," I agree. Maybe she'll let me borrow her car versus being my personal driver.

Pulling out her desk chair, she plops down and opens up her laptop. "Oh, hey, did you hear about the campus vandal? Apparently, he's bashed a statue, cut the nets at the tennis court, and the most recent thing he's been flushing entire rolls of toilet paper just to back things up." She shakes her head. "Ridiculous."

Yes, it is. This is my life now: campus vandals.

She clicks a few keys. "Just let me know when you're ready to go."

From the top bunk, I look down at the crown of her straight black hair. I bet if I asked she'd lend me her keys.

But the problem with this whole college/campus/room-mate/friend thing is that lone wolves stand out. If I don't start "belonging" I'll be looked at with suspicion.

And belonging means things like letting her drive me places. But that's okay. I'm an expert at blending in.

I jump down off the top bunk. "Okay, how about you take me to my house?"

She jumps up. "Can we stop for froyo first?"

Kill me now.

17

———————

Sabrina drives a tiny bright orange Fiat. Even if she offered me her keys I'd say no. Let's just say there's no blending in when it comes to this car.

With froyo cups for each, she cranks on Cindi Lauper and somehow manages to dance, eat froyo, and drive—all at the same time.

"You know what?" she yells over the music and the chilly wind coming in the open windows. "I have a feeling we're going to be best friends!"

I can do this. I can let her drive me around for a bit. I will not kill her.

I check my phone, hoping the mechanic has called/texted/sent a smoke signal telling me my Jeep is not so bad and will be ready later, or at most tomorrow. I need more of those espresso beans.

While I'm staring at my phone, I bring up Tommy's name to find that he's still keeping silent.

She cranks the music even louder, taking the plastic spoon from the froyo cup and using it as a microphone. "But girls they wanna have fun. Oh, girls just want to have. That's all they really want."

Yeah, I'm probably not going to survive this.

She whips around the corner that leads into my family's community before slowing her pace and letting out a long whistle. "Sa-weet."

I give my neighborhood a good long study as she rolls slowly through, and yeah, it is a pretty nice development. My parents got in when the places were going up and so they were able to pick out flooring, cabinets, and what not. The yards are tiny but each brick and siding home sprawls upward and out with a two car garage and a finished basement. Victor said the homes are roughly three thousand square feet.

In another year, Daisy will be gone to college, but somehow I don't see Victor and Justin moving. Victor will keep the house so Daisy and I have some place to come home to.

It's what he does.

I spy my stepdad just pulling into the garage and glance at the dash's clock. It's a bit past two. That's odd for him to be home. He kills the engine and with briefcase in hand, steps from the SUV.

Sabrina sighs. "Older dudes in suits get me every time." She nods in Victor's direction. "Especially ones that look like that." She looks around. "So which one is yours?"

"The older dude in the suit."

"Oh." Sabrina giggles. "Whoops."

Victor glances up as Sabrina pulls her tiny fiat into our short driveway and yanks up the emergency brake. His gaze meets mine, more than curious of the story behind this one.

Out the open driver's window, Sabrina waves. "Hi, Mr. Cameron, I'm Sabrina, Lane's roommate!"

He waves. "Hello, Sabrina, nice to meet you."

She reaches to turn off her car, and I open the door and climb out. "Well, thanks." There's no way I'm inviting her inside. I have too much stuff to do and now with Victor here that puts enough of a kink in things. I'd planned on searching his office and computer for anything he's compiled on this degraded DNA business.

"Oh...okay." Luckily, her phone rings, this time with *Wannabe*. She sighs. "My mother."

"Maybe it's important," I say.

"It's not. Believe me." With another wave she backs out, answering the phone anyway. "You all are driving me *nuts*."

I turn to Victor, and his lips twitch. "So that's the opera-loving snorer."

"Yep." I glance down at his briefcase, itching to look inside. "What are you doing home?"

"I took a personal day or rather an afternoon."

Hm, probably has to do with the exact same thing I'm here for.

Victor walks back inside the garage. "Where's your Jeep?"

"It broke down and I had it towed."

"Why didn't you call me?" He opens the interior door, and I follow him in.

"I didn't want to worry you. You've got a lot going on."

He crosses through the laundry room and into the great room to put his stuff down on the dining room table. "It's no bother. I'm your dad. It's my job to worry and help. How long until you get your Jeep back?"

"Don't know. I'm waiting to hear from the mechanic." I glance down at his SUV keys, rethinking my plans. "Are you here for your personal day or are you going back out?"

"I'm only here to change and then I'm going back out."

His phone lights up with an incoming text and he gives it a quick glance. "I really need to go. You'll be okay here? You can always do a Lyft if you need to go somewhere. Just make sure you check the license tag and ask who they're picking up."

I wave him off. "I'm okay."

"Right." He leaves everything on the dining room table and trots upstairs. As soon as his door closes, I grab his phone and swipe his lock screen—right, diagonal left, and down—and I blow out a relieved breath when his lock code hasn't changed.

I bring up his texts messages. There's a few from a fellow FBI agent. Looks like Victor is tapping into their resources after all. Quickly, I roll through them.

NO EVIDENCE YOUR WIFE, SUZIE, WAS EVER IN THE HOME.

GLORIA MICHAELS WAS THE WOMAN WHO COMMITTED SUICIDE, A SINGLE MOM.

NO EVIDENCE THE DAUGHTER WHO FOUND HER EVER EXISTED.

There's a photo of the old newspaper article attached as well. Again, something niggles around inside of me. I've seen that article before.

No evidence the daughter ever existed. Now that I didn't know. The daughter who found Gloria's body. Just like current day with the son who found his mom.

I put down Victor's phone and I reach for his briefcase. Unlike Mom's case, his is locked. I can pick this lock, but I don't have enough time.

Upstairs, his door opens, and I move from the table into the kitchen where I busy myself making a sandwich.

Two suicides. Both with children who found them. Both single moms.

Or two murders made to look like suicide. Or...two women forced to commit suicide.

Hm.

Okay, going with the forced idea, then this killer is a very different type of monster. Why the single mom, the neck cutting, the children who find them...what is the motivation for that setup?

And why forty years apart? Unless there is more in between.

A serial killer doesn't randomly do anything. There's a meaning behind it. A pattern. A ritual. Trophies taken or something left. An anniversary or a celebration. Or to grieve.

Or I'm way off here and this is truly two exact suicides at the same house precisely forty years apart.

Yeah, right.

With a little wave to me, Victor snatches up his phone and keys, leaves his briefcase right where it is and crosses through our house to the garage.

The briefcase. Perfect.

18

A s expected, it doesn't take me long to pick the lock on Victor's case. A quick glance at the clock tells me I have about thirty minutes before Daisy and Justin get home.

Inside the case lays several file folders and I glance through them, finding some work-related and not applicable. At the bottom, though, lays an unlabeled black folder and I flip it open.

Mom.

There are pictures of her parents, long since gone. School records. Military documents. Addresses where she lived. Social security documents. Information on her time with the FBI. But there's not one mention of her ever being connected to the private residence where her childhood DNA was found.

Lane, baby, do you realize who I am? Do you realize the resources I have access to? I've spent my adult life hunting people. I can certainly make one up. I know how to generate false paperwork and make it look perfect.

Mom's words trickle through my memory as I go back

over the page. "This isn't her," I whisper. She made all of this up.

Outside come Daisy and Justin's voices, returning sooner than expected. Quickly, I reassemble Victor's case, close and lock it, and I'm scrolling my phone when my brother and sister walk in.

They both come to a stop when they see me sitting at the dining room table.

"What are you doing here?" Daisy asks, and I tell her about my Jeep.

"That sucks," Justin says, and Daisy and I both smile.

Tossing his book bag in the living room, he swings into the kitchen and dives into the refrigerator. I glance out the front window and down to the curb where Daisy has parked her car, or rather the white Lexus that Mom used to drive.

I'm about to ask Daisy if I can borrow it when she says, "Justin, get your gear. Football's in thirty."

"Yeah, yeah," he says and heads upstairs.

"Football?" I ask.

"Dad agreed to it. They're doing some sort of camp in prep for next year's team."

"What? Justin doesn't even like football. Is he giving up Aikido?"

"I don't know." She checks to make sure Justin has cleared the stairs before sliding into the high-back chair beside me. She glances at Victor's briefcase.

"He came home and then left," I say. "Personal day."

She sits up. "Is he okay?"

I'm quick to assure her. After his heart attack, we're both on high alert when it comes to Victor taking it easy.

Silence falls between us as she looks at me and I look at her. I suspect she wants to know more. The last time we talked I left her hanging and she surprisingly didn't follow up. She proved to be quite the resource in tracking down Mom's old high school boyfriend. There's no telling what else she's tracked down or *can* track down.

I've spent so much time protecting her from secrets she's slowly unraveling. The fact is, my sister is stronger than I have ever given her credit for. And while I'm not ready to tell her all the darkest things about me, I am ready to share this with her. My sister is an ally. We're on the same side.

Hell, for all I know she's already dug into Mom's childhood and knows more than I realize.

"What are your plans after dropping Justin?" I ask.

"I'm all yours, sister."

19

Daisy and I dropped Justin at football and here we are at my dorm.

"Let me grab my charger," I tell her, "and I'll be right out."

She kills the engine. "I haven't seen your room yet. Plus, I just have to meet the opera adoring snorer."

"Okay, but you asked for it."

Together we walk across the student lot, round the corner of my dorm, and trot up the few steps. Whereas yesterday these steps were normal gray concrete, now they're painted with squiggly lines.

Ah, the campus vandal strikes again.

We walk inside the front door and come to an immediate halt. Residents pack the lobby, both boys and girls. Boxes, too, full of reflector vests, flashlights, and security strobes.

Conversation buzzes as everyone busies themselves trying on vests, putting batteries in flashlights, and flicking the strobes on and off.

A giant campus map sits taped to the wall with bold X's

in various colors. Beside the map are a list with times, campus zones, and student names.

Great. They've organized a student security mob. Just what every person needs who wants to come and go at all hours undetected.

"Lane!" Sabrina bounds up, all decked out in an orange vest with a strobe attached and a flashlight secured around her waist. She presses the ON button of the strobe, and Daisy and I both wince.

"Jesus," Daisy says, reaching forward and turning it right back off.

I make the introductions and Sabrina gives Daisy a big hug. "Nice to meet you!"

Sabrina waves her arm around the room. "We organized a campus watch."

Yeah, no kidding.

Sabrina snatches the flashlight off her waist and spins it like she's in a shootout in the old west. "You ready to catch the campus vandal?"

Daisy and I exchange a look.

My roommate holsters her flashlight. "You gotta be aware of everyone. Gotta know their comings and goings. Make notes. Keep track. Report if something's off." She pulls a whistle from a Velcro pocket on her vest and gives it a blow. The students gathered in the lobby echo with their own whistles.

Great, whistles too.

Sabrina nods over to the wall where the map and sign-up sheet are located. "I put your name in zone blue."

This is not happening.

She leans in. "I noticed Zach signed up for that zone, too."

"Zach?" Daisy snaps me a surprised look.

"Oh, yeah, forgot to tell you. He's enrolled here, too."

"Well, that'll be interesting," Daisy mumbles.

Sabrina bounces on the balls of her feet. "Make sure you get supplies before they run out!" With that, she twirls off.

I look over at Daisy. Her lips twitch, and I roll my eyes. College kids patrolling. Everyone reporting. No one moving around unnoticed. Including me. Who cares about the vandal? I'm more worried about the flashlight-wearing, strobe-toting, whistle-bound students. Because as long as this vandal is on the loose, I'll have no real privacy.

Clearly, I need to track this shithead down and stop him so that I can move on with my life.

s we're pulling back out of the dorm, Daisy says, "How are things with you and Tommy?"

"Good." I mean, I guess. I know it's only been a day, but I thought for sure I'd hear from him by now.

Daisy lowers the visor to cut the brightness from her eyes. "I've always been good with Justin, but lately I can't figure him out. I try to take him seriously, then I try not to. Nothing works. It's like he's this complex person now and it's not in my skill set to understand him."

From behind my sunglasses, I glance over at Daisy. "That's insightful."

"I'm trying to be a good sister and daughter, but every day since Mom died things get more complicated, not less. It's hard to juggle it all."

She's putting words to my own thoughts.

In the passenger seat, I shift to get a better look at her. I want her to know I'm really listening. "Daisy, I feel the same way. It can be overwhelming and perhaps you and I both need to realize our limitations. And we need to work at un-complicating our lives. We don't have to take everything on."

"But I want to. It's like I'm truly finding who I am now."

"Okay, I get that."

Silence falls between us then as Daisy continues driving, and shifting forward, I type an address into the GPS. My sister doesn't ask what I'm typing in. She simply follows the automated directions.

She says, "Mom's whole life was about serial killers. It was all she thought about. Why do you suppose that is?"

"I asked her that one time, and she said she lost a childhood friend to a killer who was never caught. That one single event changed the direction of her life."

"Hm."

That's all Daisy says, and it's a loaded *Hm.* It makes me think she knows something I don't.

We drive in silence after that, heading toward Alexandria. Eventually, the GPS tells Daisy to turn and that our destination is fifty yards ahead on the right.

Yellow police tape sections off the small brick house and I spy an unmarked car parked several spots up and on the left side. "Pull over the first chance you get."

She parallel parks between a truck and a small two-door, and together we stare at the tiny home surrounded by police tape.

"A woman was found a couple of days ago in that house. Bled out from a sliced open neck. Apparent suicide. Forty years ago the exact same thing happened in that exact house. Our mom may have witnessed it."

Daisy snaps me a surprised look. "What are you talking about?"

"I overheard Victor on the phone. They found a degraded sample of her DNA that puts her in the house when she was five years old. And it could all coincide. That's what I'm trying to figure out."

I allow a few beats of silence to go by while Daisy goes back to looking at the house and digesting what I just said.

"Only I'm not sure it was suicide. We could be talking about murder."

Daisy looks over at me again.

Something in her eyes makes a nervous swallow work its way down my throat. I'm not supposed to bring Daisy into this world, but here I am—doing just that. "I've decided to really dig in. I have a theory the killer either made it look like a suicide or forced the women to do it."

"A suicide killer?" Daisy whispers.

The Suicide Killer—an apt name for sure. "An entirely different monster, and with forty years between the two kills, there are likely more. There has to be a pattern, a motivation, a ritual."

This time, she's the one who swallows.

I keep going, "You're better with computers than me. Perhaps you can help me do some digging?"

Another few beats go by as she looks at me and I look at her. Then she takes her sunglasses from the console and slips them on. She doesn't want me seeing her eyes. I don't like that, but I respect it.

"A forty-year span of killings," Daisy says. "A person who possibly talks people into committing suicide. That's impressive in a disturbing and evil way. I wonder if this ever hit on Mom's radar."

Daisy's words flitter through my brain, sparking a repressed image. Yes, I knew I had seen that old newspaper article before. It's in Mom's files.

An excited twitch moves through me. We moved Mom's files to the basement. Which is exactly where I'm going as soon as I get a chance. "If I'm right on this, he's likely a loner. Obsessed with suicide. With forty years spanning, he would be older. Maybe even sixty or seventy? The only thing that really gets his heart beating is the act. Likely not to look at his object as prey. He (or she) has come back to this house for a reason. This area might be home—"

"It's like being in the car with Mom. Serial killers intrigue you as much as they did her. She'd get a whiff of a bad guy and we'd never see her."

I hate that she just compared me to Mom, but it's the truth. I get the whiff of a bad guy and my whole world clicks into place.

"I'd say let's go inside and have a look around—" She nods to the unmarked car— "But with that car over there, an investigator is inside."

I should be surprised Daisy knows that's an unmarked car, but at this point, nothing about my sister is shocking me.

"Why don't we just ask Dad about all of this?" Daisy asks.

"I'd rather keep it between us."

"We're keeping a lot of stuff from Dad and just between you and me." Daisy puts the Lexus in gear and as she does, something about her demeanor changes. She's gone from nervous to approachable to now being irritated. "You know what, I don't like secrets. And I don't want to be here. I'm not intrigued by killers like you and Mom are."

She pulls away from the curb, and the gap that used to be between us is there again. Sisters in name only. I made a mistake bringing her here. Why did I just say all of that? Why am I trying to pull her into my world?

21

S abrina signed me up for the ten to eleven shift in zone blue which covers the library, the student center, and the tennis courts.

Really, I could care less about this vandal situation, but the quicker I find him, the quicker this irritation is over and I can move on to more important things like digging into Mom's files.

The only bright spot is that Sabrina signed me up next to Zach's name. At least I'm patrolling with someone I like.

"Halt!" Someone yells and I close my eyes. You've got to be kidding me.

Turning around, I watch Sabrina jog toward me decked out in all black with her bright orange vest.

Giggling, she comes to a stop in front of me. "I knew that was you. I was just kidding."

"What are you doing?"

She looks at my jeans and hoodie. "Where's your gear?"

I wave that off. "I'm fine. Why are you here? I thought you were patrolling at a different time."

"Zach had something come up and needed a fill in." She

snaps to attention and salutes. "I'm the fill in." She grins. "This'll be fun."

"Yeah, fun."

She digs a pack of gum from her pocket and pops one in. "So I was thinking about how you and Zach used to date. And then he left. And you moved on. And he probably moved on to. And now he's back. And you didn't know he was back. And being your high school boyfriend you probably loved him. And boy is that confusing." Blowing a bubble, she looks at me. "Ya know?"

This girl is going to be the death of me.

Sister, daughter, roommate, student, girlfriend. It was a hell of a lot easier when Mom was alive. I rarely had to deal with anybody. Now, someone is always there. There's no escape. And Sabrina's right. Now Zach is back. Is that good or bad? I have no clue.

Putting things in perspective, it's pretty lame I'm complaining about people wanting to be with me.

From her back pocket, Sabrina's phone plays *Macarena*. She waves it off. "My grandmother. I'll get it later." She cuts off between the shadowed area between the library and the student center. She points to the side entrance of the student center. "Need to pee. Be right back."

She uses her student ID card and beeps into the building. While I wait for her, I take a look around the shadowed area between the two buildings. I could leave, but that wouldn't be too roommate-friendly of me.

In my periphery, I catch sight of someone running. Or more like darting from shadow to shadow, and my senses prick to alert. Hello, Mr. Vandal.

I take off after him.

Dressed in all black, he (or she) wears a full-face ski mask and holds a spray paint can in his right hand. Ah, hard at work. He's small and slender, making me lean more toward the vandal being a girl versus a boy. Either way, my target will be easy to take down.

I'm going to scare the piss out of this idiot.

He ducks around the corner of a brick building, disappearing even more into the darkness and I pick up the pace. I don't care I'm not wearing a disguise. This isn't a disguise type of event.

The sound of a spray can filters through the night and I follow it. The vandal stands with his back to me as he paints a poor attempt of a large white skull on the side of a classroom building.

I stand several feet back, my head cocked, studying his technique. I'll let him finish and then I'll make my move.

While he hurriedly completes his ridiculous art, he glances over his right shoulder, then his left, not even spotting me right behind him. Finally, he's done, tosses the can down, spins around to run, and his eyes widen when he sees me.

"Hello," I say.

Wildly, he looks around, backing up.

I sigh. "I wouldn't run if I were you. And I wouldn't fight. Believe me, when I say, I'll win."

His breathing accelerates, and now that I'm looking more at his slender and short body, this might be a kid, not a college student.

"I don't really care who you are," I say. "But you need to stop breaking things, cutting tennis nets, painting random stuff, and being an all-around pain in the ass. If I see you back here again, I won't be so reasonable."

"Oh, whatever!" The vandal shouts. "I'm not scared of you."

I move lightning quick, shoving the miscreant up against

the wall that he just painted. Cramming my arm under his throat, I force his head up as I glare down into his charcoal-rimmed eyes.

He tries to throw a side punch, but I sense the shift in weight in time to grab his wrist. He's stronger than expected and I press his wrist into the brick wall beside his hip. I shift my weight closer, making sure he's completely pinned and unable to try another punch or a kick.

"You need to calm the hell down," I say.

He glares at me, more pissed I've pinned him then he is I caught him vandalizing the campus.

I wish I had a hand free to yank his hood off.

But I stay right where I am, waiting him out. It's just like working with animals. Show them who is alpha and they'll eventually submit.

Another few beats go by while I stare at him and he stares at me, and as expected, he looks away first. But still, I don't move. When his body releases, then I'll know he's fully submitted.

He sighs then, and with it, the tension in his shoulders ease. Good, that's what I was waiting on—the realization of defeat.

Still, though, I don't move. Something tells me this is a good kid who's making bad choices.

He sighs again. "It's me," he whispers.

It takes me a second to register what he just said, and when his words filter in, I shove away from him and the wall and I yank his hood off. "Justin? What the hell!"

Tears well in his eyes, filling up and tipping over to trail through the charcoal he smeared over his face. "I'm sorry," he mumbles, and with a sniff, he wipes the back of his hand under his nose. "Please don't tell Dad."

"You have got to tell me what's going on, and how did you even get here?"

"I snuck out. Dad thinks I'm in bed. One of my friends has an older brother who drives. They picked me up. They're waiting on me."

"What do you mean they're waiting on you? Did they tell you to do this?"

"No," he whispers. "It was my idea."

I look down at his ski mask still gripped in my hand. "Justin, you're going to have to spell this out for me. I really don't understand what's going on. This isn't you."

The tears come in full force, and I fight everything in me to comfort him. He needs to face what he's done.

"Th-there's a group at school and they're really popular. They started being nice to me. Th-they want me to be their friend. But they've been mean to some other kids. I tried to be mean, too, b-but I can't."

"So you thought if you came here and vandalized this campus, it'd make you look cool so you don't have to look cool by picking on other kids?"

With a sniff, he nods and I don't know what to say. I have never once wanted to belong to a group. I don't get the whole peer-pressure thing. "Justin, you know this is wrong. I don't have to tell you that. You can't and shouldn't do this. You know better. This thing you're going through, it's over."

He brings his wet eyes up to mine. "Please don't tell Dad."

I look down into his charcoal smeared face that isn't so little boy anymore. He's going to be a teenager soon and then an adult. I take no joy in ratting him out to Victor, but in this case, I believe it's necessary.

My brother is at one of those forks in the road and he's choosing the wrong prong. I always thought Justin was more like me, but in this moment, he's more like Daisy. This is exactly what she would have done. She would have been mean to someone just to belong and would have defaced property just to appear cool.

Back when she was this age, I didn't care. She did her thing, and I did mine.

Well, I'm not making that mistake again. I will not allow a gap to form between me and Justin.

"Is this why you're suddenly interested in football, too?"

He shrugs. "Maybe."

Sabrina runs around the side of the classroom building and skids to a halt. Her gaze goes from me to Justin, to the skull graffiti, down to the spray paint can, and over to the ski mask that I ripped off his head.

"Um... you're just a kid." She points at Justin. "He's just a kid."

For a brief second, I debate not telling her Justin is my brother, but if I don't, she'll haul him off to campus security.

I take a few steps away, nodding her over for privacy, and when we're out of earshot, I lower my voice. "His name is Justin, and he's my brother. Without going into a lot of detail, my family has not had the easiest of times lately. Can you please let me handle this at home?"

Folding her arms, she glances through the shadows back to where Justin stands looking at the ground. "I suppose we can make something up. Or for that matter, as long as the vandalizing stops, the whole thing will eventually be forgotten." She looks back at me. "Okay, it'll be our secret."

Great. Now I'm sharing secrets with Sabrina.

22

Sabrina took me and Justin home. I woke Victor up and while Justin sulked, I told my stepdad the whole thing. I slept in my old room, and in the morning I find Victor packing for a trip.

"What's going on?" I ask, stepping into the master bedroom.

He glances up as he zips up a duffel bag. "I'm taking Daisy and Justin away for a few days. I've already called both of their schools to tell them. We need family time. You're welcome to come, but you have classes you can't skip. And, of course, Patch and Paw." He shrugs. "Up to you."

I try not to show him how excited this news makes me. I'll have the whole place to myself for several uninterrupted days.

But I do give him my best bummed expression. "Yeah, unfortunately, I can't. My Jeep will be ready later today. I have work and classes I definitely can't skip. Especially chemistry."

"All good, but please get caught up on your sleep. I worry about you."

"I will."

Carrying his duffel bag, he scoots past me, and if I knew how to do an Irish jig, I'd do one right now. This is going to be awesome. I fully intend on making the most of their trip without me.

Several minutes later, I stand outside, waving goodbye to the three of them and ignoring Justin's scowl from the back seat of the SUV. Hopefully, he'll return as the brother he used to be.

Instead, I focus on Daisy's stoic expression as she stares at me from the passenger side. I've had that look. She's pulling away from me. I miscalculated. She's not ready to know more.

All I can do is give her space and not lie when she comes back to me. All Mom did was lie to me and I will not do that to Daisy.

I give her a slight smile to let her know I love her, and when the SUV cruises through the neighborhood and out of sight, I go back inside.

First order of business—Tommy. He still hasn't called me and it's beyond time we spoke. Then I'll rifle through the files in the basement.

As I walk back inside, I dial his number. He picks up on the first ring. "I was wondering when you would call me."

"And I was wondering when you would call me. So what's up with you and the biker gang?" I do like to get right to the point.

"I hate that you saw me."

"Why?"

"Because...because..." He sighs.

I need to put him out of his misery. "I know all about the BDAP, and if you're part of that, then that's cool. You don't have to explain anything to me."

A long pause follows, and I use the time to make a cup of coffee.

Finally, he says, "So now you know my secret."

"I do."

"Bad people come in all shapes and sizes, and sometimes they're the very people we're supposed to trust. Like social workers."

And parents. "Is that who you were there for, a social worker?" Of course, I already know the answer to this, but he doesn't know that.

"Yes. And what were you doing out there?" he asks.

I knew this was coming and so I'm ready. "I was lost. My lab partner lives out there and I couldn't find his place."

"Oh."

He doesn't believe me, but I'm sticking to it.

Another long pause follows, and I use the time to make oatmeal.

"What about you, Lane? What's a secret you're keeping?"

Yeah, I'm not going there with Tommy. Not now, at least.

He continues, "I want to know more of what's going on inside of you."

No, he doesn't. But he won't be satisfied unless I tell him something and so I say, "Zach is back."

Another long pause and I use the time to load the dishwasher. Maybe that information wasn't what Tommy wanted.

Finally, he says, "Okay, and?"

"And nothing. Just thought you should know, seeing as how you're my boyfriend and you also know my history with Zach and his older brother."

More of the awkward pausing, and I use the time to eat the oatmeal I made. I'm not used to this from Tommy. Is he jealous? Is he leery that I know his BDAP secret?

"Your voice is different when you talk about Zach and his brother."

Hm, I didn't realize. I suppose so, though. "There's nothing to be jealous about."

"I didn't say I was."

But he is.

Yet more silence stretches between us, and I finish my oatmeal, rinse the bowl, and put it into the dishwasher. "What's up with all the awkward pauses? Don't make me fill in your thoughts."

"I don't know. You never quite say the things I think you're going to say. That's all."

"Well, snap out of it. This isn't you and me. We talk. Just say what you want to say."

"You're doing something to me, and I don't know what it is. I thought I could keep my feelings for you at this slow sort of hum, like background noise. But the more I'm around you, the more my feelings become dangerous."

"Dangerous?"

"As in you could ruin me," he softly admits.

I pause in my kitchen chores. "Tommy... I don't know how to respond to that. I would never intentionally hurt you. You know that, right?"

Another stretch of silence, but this time I don't move, I wait. And wait. And wait. Jesus Christ, he's killing me with these pauses. "Tommy?"

"That's just it, I see you eventually hurting me and not realizing it. You wouldn't mean to. You wouldn't have intent. But it would just happen. I'm more invested in this than you, and it scares me."

Somewhere deep in my gut, nerves squirm. Is he breaking up with me before we've even really started? That is the last thing I want, and frankly, I didn't know he felt this deeply for me. I thought we were on the same go-as-it-flows page.

But I want Tommy in my life. I do care if he ends things. I'm not indifferent. Clearly, I need to show this. Speaking the words isn't enough. He needs to know that Zach being back means just that—Zach is back. I'm not confused. I want to be with Tommy.

"Are you free tonight?" I ask.

"I am."

"Let's hang out. Yes? I'll come to you."

"Okay." With that, he clicks off. No goodbye. No see ya later. Nothing.

He didn't even sound excited.

My phone buzzes with a text and I quickly look at the screen, hoping it's Tommy. Zach's name pops up instead. HEY, THINKING OF YOU AND WANTED TO SAY HI.

I stare at that message long and hard, probably too long. Had it come in before my conversation with Tommy, I'd likely think nothing of it. Now, though, I give it entirely too much thought.

In my head I compose several texts back:

HI BACK.

CLASSES GOING OKAY?

I NEED A RIDE TO PICK UP MY JEEP.

But in the end, I don't reply and instead, I turn the phone over so I can't see the screen. Tommy is my boyfriend. I care for him. I won't screw that up. I'm not sure what that means when it comes to Zach, but right now it means I'm not responding to his text.

23

I use the few available hours I have to dive into the degraded DNA and my thoughts that the suicides might, in fact, be murders.

The first place I go to is Victor's office, but unlike Mom, he doesn't leave things accessible. He rarely if ever brings work home.

Still, though, I search his work area, coming up with the same thing I had before from his briefcase.

Next, I head to the basement where we moved Mom's boxes. I grab the first one labeled OFFICE and dive in. Most of this I've already picked through, looking for anything on Mom's alter ego, The Decapitator, my real father, and Aunt Marji. I pulled a few things, but Mom did a good job of keeping her extra-curricular activities off the radar.

Yes, the last time I looked through these files, I wasn't searching for information on suicides being linked to a possible serial murderer. I do remember that newspaper clipping though...

It takes me thirty minutes and twenty or so files to find it. It's in a folder labeled GHOSTS and I assume that means things that haunt her, or cases never solved, or personal interests not brought before the FBI.

Personal interests. Much like my journals of research on serial killers.

The thick folder contains photos, police reports, newspaper clippings, and memo pads with her personal views. From what I can tell, it covers a variety of killers, or rather *ghosts* to be solved.

I don't see anything on suicides, though.

An eight-by-ten white envelope sits tucked in with everything else. Opening the clasp, I pour the contents out onto the carpet, and, bingo—I find exactly what I'm looking for: information on suicides tracing back through the years. Hangings, slit wrists, overdose, gunshot, and various other methods.

Mom suspected something, too.

I find several spreadsheets where she's analyzed things by hand, cross-checking by type of suicide, time of year, location, the victim, and miscellaneous other things. Faded pencil marks are visible where she's circled and erased, probably thinking there was a pattern, then deciding not.

At first inspection, I don't see one either.

I can almost visualize her meticulously marking these sheets, and as I study them I recall all the times she used to tape things to her office walls.

"Why do you do that?" I asked.

"Because I like to stand back and see my thoughts from different angles."

Remembering that conversation has me getting up off the floor. I find scotch tape in one of her office boxes and tape the spreadsheets on the basement wall. I stand back several paces, carefully scrutinizing the multiple rows and columns. I begin to see it—the tiny penciled dots she placed in certain squares of the spreadsheet.

My gaze moves vertically, then horizontally, and as I do the other places on the sheets fade to only the squares with the tiny dots.

I grab a yellow legal pad and a pencil and notate:

- New Orleans
    - November 10: single mother, found by child, bled out
    - November 13: single mother, found by child, overdose
    - November 15: single mother, found by child, hanging
- Memphis
    - November 10: single mother, found by child, bled out
    - November 13: single mother, found by child, overdose
    - November 15: single mother, found by child, hanging
- Chicago
    - November 10: single mother, found by child, bled out
    - November 13: single mother, found by child, overdose
    - November 15: single mother, found by child, hanging
- Portland
    - November 10: single mother, found by child, bled out
    - November 13: single mother, found by child, overdose
    - November 15: single mother, found by child, hanging

A SENSE of black wonder drifts through me that this killer has successfully been pulling this off—year after year after year.

On and on it goes. Every year in November, the exact same pattern, each time in a new city. No repeats, which means the Suicide Killer has a traveling job. A truck driver? A salesman? Self-employed? Online work?

Hard to say. There are a lot of remote jobs now.

No repeated cities until now. Why?

Going with the pattern November 10, 13, 15 means tonight (November 13) there will be a suicide by overdose of a single mom found by her child.

Where, though? And does this possibly connect to Mom's degraded DNA?

For some reason the killer has come back to Northern Virginia, specifically Alexandria. If I can just figure out where tonight's overdose will occur, then maybe I can stop this from happening and even better, catch the son of a bitch.

I kneel down on the carpet and thumb through the GHOSTS file. There are no personal notations of Mom's. Only facts. She kept her feelings to herself. If she is connected to this, she didn't want anyone knowing it.

Finding the old article of the house with the bled out woman, I lay that aside. I sift through the other materials, looking for anything else forty years ago in Alexandria, and I find an obituary of a young woman who overdosed. Body found in a car in an Alexandria park.

Though which park it doesn't say. If I can just figure out which one...

I glance back up to the wall with the taped spreadsheets and something powerful shifts in me, like pieces of a puzzle clicking into place. I'm close to figuring this out, and I will. Between the overdose that will occur tonight and the hanging two days from now, I will figure this out.

Mom couldn't. She was either too close to the case, she wasn't able to forecast this killer's movements, or there's some other reason. He's back in this area, which according to her notes, she didn't predict either. But I now have the advantage of knowing.

I keep staring at the sheets. Why are you so successful? How do you get the single mother to do it, or how do you make it look like she did it? How is it the child is the one who finds her? Why doesn't the child know a murder has occurred? Why the pattern of a woman bled out, one overdose, and the last a hanging? How is this personally connected to you, the Suicide Killer?

I glance back down to the reports and photos, again looking for anything in Alexandria forty years ago. A penciled sketch catches my attention and I slide it out. It's a woman hanging from a tree.

Mom wasn't a artist and so this had to have been done by an actual sketch artist, though I'm not sure where this would have come from. Perhaps a reporter on the scene? Either way, in the bottom corner Mom has scrawled a few notes:

November 15, hanging, off of Parkway

Meaning the G. W. Parkway that runs along the Potomac. I study the sketch, trying to gauge the surroundings. There's a boat in the background, tied up to a dock. An old marina perhaps? The water behind it spans deep and wide with land on the other side.

But this is a forty-year-old sketch and who knows what it looks like now.

It's Alexandria, though, and so that narrows things.

But let's focus on the overdose tonight. Grabbing my phone, I type in a few searches on the obituary and get back nothing of significance. I do find one mention of the child who forty years ago found his mom. An eight-year-old boy named Frederick Thurmont. He'd be 48 years old now.

I do a search on Frederick Thurmont, Alexandria, Virginia and get back two hits. One a history teacher and the other a manager of a grocery store, both on Facebook. I have no clue if the Frederick Thurmont I'm looking for still lives in Alexandria, but it's the best I've got. I pull up their public profiles. Given the timeline of him being 48 now, that matches the grocery store manager.

It's Safeway Grocery on U.S. 1 and I dial the number. As it connects I put Mom's things back in order.

"Safeway Grocery, may I help you?"

I clear my throat. "Yes, I'm looking for Frederick Thurmont."

"Hold please."

Musak comes on as I un-tape the spreadsheets from the wall.

"This is Mr. Thurmont, may I help you?"

I hadn't quite thought of what to say, but I go with whatever pops into my head. "Yes, hello, my name is Maggie Cain and I'm with the Division of Electronic Media and Census Bureau out of New York." I have no clue if that even exists, but it sounds good. "I'm tracking suicide rates over the last fifty years and I have here your mother committed suicide forty years ago in Alexandria, Virginia. She overdosed?"

Silence.

"Hello, Mr. Thurmont?"

"Yes," he quietly says. "That's correct."

"This is a sensitive subject and I do apologize. I'll be quick. If you could just tell me where this occurred?"

He clears his throat. "Fort Hunt."

"And you were the one who found her?"

He sighs. "Yes."

"And where were you at the time?"

"In the car. Asleep in the back. I woke up and—well, found her."

I hate I'm causing this man pain, but I have to if I'm going to stop this. "Again, I do apologize. Just one last question. Do you remember anything before that?"

"What do you mean?"

I want to ask if there was another person present but I don't want to set off any alarms. "How did you come to be in the car?"

"I don't know. It was late. I was in bed for the night. Mom probably put me in the car. It was a long time ago and not something I want to recall, so I'm hoping you're satisfied with your answers?"

"Oh, yes, thank you. You have been most helpful."

We click off and I sit for a minute thinking. Asleep in the car. Woke up and found her. That matches the one from a few days ago. The child woke from a nap and found her.

I go back to the file I was just organizing and quickly sift through the notes. *Child was sleeping in the next room. Daughter woke the next morning. Son slumbering right beside her.*

Does he drug the kids? Most likely. That would explain how the children never see or hear the actual killing, but wake to find the aftermath.

Assuming the Suicide Killer was in his twenties forty years ago, he'd be in his sixties now, maybe seventies.

Whichever, this person is very smart. Suicides are not investigated like homicides.

Except my mom was onto the pattern. Yet couldn't quite piece it together or move fast enough to catch him. Or perhaps she chose not to catch him. She wanted to study his methods.

Or maybe, just maybe, she was scared of him. Now that's an intriguing thought.

Mom was a serial killer, yes, but she also devoted her life to hunting other killers down. I'm sure she looked at them as worthy adversaries, especially these ghosts left un-hunted.

Every serial killer is a jigsaw puzzle with pieces to assemble, and when all the ends are connected, the picture of motivation perfectly forms.

The Suicide Killer is a monster, and his path quite possibly crossed my mother's when she was just a little girl. If she witnessed his crime, why did he let her live? Why was

Mom there? What is her connection to the woman who died? I may not know all the answers, but I do know where this killer most likely will be tonight.

Fort Hunt.

I put her boxes back in the closet, gather all the information on the suicides, and walk upstairs from the basement. The alarm on my phone beeps with a reminder it's time to pick up my Jeep. Perfect.

Family comes first. That thought drove hard into me when Victor had his heart attack and ended up in the hospital. But just because Mom's degraded DNA was found in a house linked to all of this doesn't mean it's the driving force behind finding the Suicide Killer. She might be my family, but she does not come first. Not anymore.

For some reason, this killer has come back to Alexandria. Serendipity? We'll go with that for now.

As I walk outside to wait on my Lyft, another thought filters in: Is this Suicide Killer responsible for the evil my mother became? Did he create her?

Daisy doesn't want into my world. She's not fascinated with killers like I am. I wish I was different, if anything, for her. But I don't want to be. This part of me, I wouldn't know who to be without it.

I would explode.

The Suicide Killer is a loner, unable to connect emotionally unless it's a victim. He doesn't deviate from his pattern, his ritual. November 10, 13, and 15. Single mothers found by a child. Cutting, overdose, hanging. What happened to bring this on?

Mom chased this person. She tracked his movements. She was fascinated by him. It's almost poetic—one serial killer chasing another.

If she were still alive would she be excited to know he was back in Alexandria? Yes, she would.

Did this killer know my mom was chasing him? Most likely not. If he did, though, would he consider her an obstacle or an admirable opponent?

An obstacle, for sure. Only someone like my mother would look at another killer as an admirable opponent.

If only Mom would have used her darkness for good. She could have focused on the killers that she chased and taken her aggression out on them and not so many innocent lives.

From her detailed spreadsheets, the Suicide Killer was her lifelong project. And now he is mine. I have tonight and two days from now and then that's it. He'll be moving on. Another city. Another wave of suicide kills next November.

He's the perfect predator camouflaged among society, scoping out the next victim, waiting for her to fit his perfect profile, and then he strikes.

Yes, if history repeats itself, he'll be at Fort Hunt tonight.

Which still leaves me with Mom's degraded DNA and what put her in that house all those years ago.

If she were alive, I would come right out and ask her, but that's not an option.

Reggie is though.

24

I've known Reggie since I was a little girl. We met at summer camp and just clicked. It's a cliché thing to say but it really did happen that way. We simply got each other.

I'm in my Jeep now on the way to Fort Hunt where I'm 99.9% sure there will be another suicide/murder. As I drive, I prop my phone in the dash mounted holder. I'm about to dial Reggie, but then I stop.

Asking her for help is what drove a wedge between us the last time. No, that's not true. Lying to her is what drove a wedge.

But she is the one person who can worm her way around cyberspace and get the information I need on the degraded DNA and the circumstances surrounding my mom being in that house.

As long as I'm honest with her, or as honest as I can be, this should be fine. This is about Mom, not me. Reggie loved my mother.

I send her a quick voice text: CAN YOU FACETIME?

YES, BUT IT HAS TO BE QUICK. I'M HEADING TO CLASS.

She answers a second later, and her pretty face fills the screen. The last time we facetimed she had shaved her head and a bit of dark curly hair has grown out since. Snow dots the ground around her as she walks across MIT's campus.

With fingerless gloves, she waves at me. "Yo."

"Yo, back."

"What's wrong?" She presses an earbud into her right ear. "I can tell by your face that something is wrong."

I take a breath. "A few days ago there was a woman found in a house in Alexandria, Virginia. She had committed suicide by slicing her own neck."

"Jesus." Reggie cringes.

"The techs who cleaned up the area found a degraded DNA sample that belonged to my mom."

"What the hell?"

"As in my mom was just a kid."

"But your mom didn't grow up in that area. Why would her childhood DNA be there?"

"I don't know."

Reggie steps around a clump of students. "Did you talk to Victor?"

"Not really. There's other stuff going on that I can fill you in on later. Stuff with Justin and Daisy. Victor's got a lot on his plate. He knows about the degraded DNA, but I don't think he has much time to really look into it right now."

She nods. "What can I do?"

"I'm sorry, Reggie, I'm aware this is what caused our fight before."

"It's okay. We're over that. This is your mom and your family. I care. This isn't one of your killers that you research."

To that, I don't respond. It's sort of fifty-fifty, so we'll call it a half-truth.

Reggie says, "Let me dig around. Text me the address in Alexandria and anything else you might have."

I sigh, so relieved she didn't shut me out. "You should know that I've already been doing my own digging."

Her lips twitch. "You wouldn't be my Lane if you weren't already investigating."

"I discovered there was a similar suicide that happened at that exact house forty years ago."

"Weird." She stops walking. "I'm here and I need to go in. Text me everything and when I get out of class, I'll start plowing away. But Lane?"

"Yeah?"

"No secrets, okay? We're best friends and best friends don't have secrets."

"No secrets," I say.

God, it's like a family curse. Lying comes way too easy for me.

25

A s I turn off down the road that borders Fort Hunt, I glance to the left where a row of small houses sits. It didn't connect in my brain until just now, but the brick home where the suicide occurred is in this neighborhood too.

WHAT TIME TONIGHT ARE YOU COMING OVER? Tommy texts.

Crap. I glance at my clock. It's half past six. I wish I could cancel. Especially if tonight turns out productive. But that's the last thing I need to do. I voice text back, NINE OKAY?

YES. SEE YOU THEN...

To the right runs a chain link fence that borders Fort Hunt. Off in the distance sits the old historic fort and over to the left a pavilion with bathrooms and picnic tables. A biking and jogging path runs the perimeter of the park. It appears to be a safe, family oriented park. I imagine a few hours ago when the sun was still up that this place was busy.

Now, though, with dusk settled in, the area has a few stragglers—a cyclist, a couple sitting on a blanket, an older man walking across the dry grass.

I continue following the road, curving around, and I slow down when cop cars, yellow police tape, and an ambulance come into view.

I pull way over and park along the edge, staring through the chain link fence. It already happened. The Suicide Killer was here.

Across the road and over to the left, a few of the homeowners venture out to see. I roll my window down to hear what they're saying.

But none of them are talking. I'm not sure they even know.

I go back to looking at the scene. A young girl sits in the back of a cop car, wrapped in a blanket and staring at the Subaru as the paramedics pull her mother from the driver's side. She woke up and found her mother dead. Overdose.

This is a fresh scene, though. It just happened. The killer may still be here.

I study the park again and the stragglers. In the distance stands the cyclist, one foot on a pedal and one on the ground as he takes in what's going on. Some yards away from him the couple gets up off the blanket to look as well. I move past them to the man who was walking across the grass. Now he's up on what's left of the relic fort, looking down at the parking lot and the scene. He's an average-sized man with a thick flannel jacket, a beanie, and khaki pants.

Of the stragglers, he'd be the one. I dig under my seat for my binoculars to get a better look. But by the time I find them and get them focused, the man is gone.

I go on instinct and follow.

I'm not entirely sure how to get around the other side of the park, but I put my Jeep in gear and roll forward. About a half mile up sits the entrance, now blocked by a cop car. I keep going, but the road dumps out onto the Parkway.

I turn right, hoping to circle around the backside of the fort and end up further down the Parkway. Exiting as soon as I can, I backtrack and get a little lost.

On foot, the mystery man may have easily crossed through Fort Hunt and vanished out the back. He knew exactly the route to disappear.

Two days from now the last suicide/murder will occur. A woman will be hung. Now I just need to figure out where. Where along the Parkway did it happen forty years ago? Because if his pattern holds, he'll be there to finish the cycle.

So will I, and this time in plenty of time to catch him.

26

I do a U-Turn, leaving Alexandria and taking the Parkway back toward McLean and my date with Tommy. I'm early, but I don't think he'll mind. I'm almost to my exit when a call comes in. It's Zach, and I consider not answering but do instead.

"Zach, you should probably know that I have a boy—"

"I'm the reason why your mother is dead. She never would have been anywhere near this house if it wasn't for me."

Turning on my blinker, I take my exit. "Zach, what happened to my mother is not your fault. You had no control over it. Where are you?"

"Bad things just happen. Is that the answer to all of this?"

"Zach, are you at the house where they found you and my mom?"

"Yes," he whispers.

"Stay there. I'm on my way."

I pass right by the road to Tommy's and head toward the interstate. I should call him, but I send him a quick voice text instead. SORRY, GOING TO BE LATE. There's no way I can make it to Zach and back by nine.

My mom, The Decapitator, killed Tommy's sister. She also had Zach strapped to a table, ready to kill him, too. Her actions have forever linked me to these two guys. As happy as I was to see Zach, I wish he would have stayed away. Coming back has thrown a kink into my already twisty life.

From McLean, it takes me roughly forty-five minutes to reach the house in Gaithersburg. This is the first home Victor and Mom owned. When we moved to McLean, they kept it as a rental property. But after everything that happened here, Victor sold it.

I don't know who lives there now. Frankly, with what happened, I wouldn't have bought the place. But to each their own and all that.

I find Zach standing on the dimly lit sidewalk staring at an empty lot. I guess the people who bought it, cleared it. Smart. I would have, too. I parallel park on the street, and I wave to a family playing night time football in their front yard. The mom cuts Zach a look, I'm sure leery of him just standing here under a street light and staring. Hopefully, my arrival will alleviate her worry.

Quietly, I step up beside him. "Hey," I softly say.

He doesn't look at me. "It's gone. It's like it never happened."

I look at the empty lot with the giant dumpster full of debris. Thank God.

"You've got a family left. A father, a sister, a brother. I hope you realize how lucky you are. Don't take any of it for granted."

"I won't. I don't."

"I was the messed up one in my family. The drinker. The

problem. Why am I the one still alive? It doesn't make sense."

I turn to him. "Don't say that."

"It doesn't matter what I do. What I choose. There's something about me that gets it wrong. Every time. I'm the problem. I hurt everyone around me. I'm broken inside."

I reach out to touch him, and he steps away. "Zach, what are you talking about?"

Shaking his head, he grinds the palms of his hands into his eyes. "Dad didn't want me to come back here."

"Why don't we go somewhere else?" I cast a look across the street to the mom who is getting her family inside. I give her a slight wave to let her know everything is okay. The last thing we need is her calling the cops.

Zach turns on me with angry eyes. "How can you stand here so calm?" He jabs a finger at the empty lot. "Your mom died there!"

I try to touch him again, but he steps away.

"Don't!" He snaps. "Have you even cried for her loss?"

Zach is in so much pain, and I can't do anything about it. He's lashing out. I get it. "Of course I've grieved."

"I thought coming here would help me make sense of it all." He paces away, leaving the glow of the streetlight and stepping into the shadows. With his back to me, he stops.

I wait, barely breathing, not sure what to do. His head drops. His breath stutters, and my heart breaks. I go to him, wrapping my arms around him, and this time he doesn't fight my touch.

His sobs come deep and mournful, and I hold him tight. "I got you."

27

H ours later after I see Zach safely back to campus, I knock on Tommy's door. It swings inward.

I open my mouth to apologize for being so late when he holds up his phone.

"Sorry, going to be late." He reads me back my text. "Thanks for the impersonal message."

"Tommy."

He shakes his head. "At first I thought, oh, she'll be fifteen minutes late. Then thirty. But one hour ticked into another, ticked into another, and nothing. I started thinking, 'Is she okay?', 'Was she in an accident?', 'Where is she?', 'Who is she with?'

But I didn't want to call you because I don't want to be that type of boyfriend. So I waited for you to call me, but apparently, you're not that type of girlfriend. I must have gotten on and off of my bike twenty times, talking myself in and out of looking for you. This is not who I am. You have put me in this position. What the hell is the explanation? You were supposed to be here at nine and it is now almost midnight."

"I'm sorry," I say. "I was with Zach."

"Of course you were."

"It's not what you think. I'm not hiding anything from you." Well, except for the fact I stalk and kill bad guys.

"I've been sitting here thinking about you for hours, and I've come to a conclusion."

I sigh. "What's that?"

"The most disturbing thing about you is how good of a liar you really are."

"Tommy."

He holds his hand up, shaking his head. "I need space."

With that, he closes the door in my face, and I turn away. What is wrong with me? Why didn't I pick up the phone and call him?

The next morning my phone buzzes with a text from Reggie: NOTHING YET. BUT...THERE IS SOMETHING THERE. IT'S BURIED DEEP.

I knew it. I thought I had put all of Mom's secrets to rest, but of course, something else is there.

28

I go through my day with classes and my Patch and Paw shift, making extra sure to check and double check the list Dr. O'Neal gave me.

I don't see Zach around campus and I don't see Sabrina either. It's my last night of freedom. Victor will be back tomorrow with Daisy and Justin and I'll be back in the dorm with no sleep.

I spread all of my things out on the dining room table, my focus solely on where the hanging occurred forty years ago. I have the sketch of the tree and the old boat taken from Mom's file, and I lay it on the table beside my laptop.

Hours go by as I dig through the internet, searching for anything I can find and coming up with nothing—not even the name of the woman who died or the child who found her. All I have is the sketch. I finally locate the artist who did it. Then I do a little digging on him to find he passed away ten years ago.

With a sigh, I sit back and close my eyes. Think, Lane, think. The first suicide/murder occurred in that neighborhood near Fort Hunt. The second inside of Fort Hunt. So logic would tell me the hanging will be nearby as well.

On a new surge, I pull up a map of the Parkway near the fort. According to the sketch, the hanging occurred on the water along the Parkway. I zoom in on a map of that area and carefully study the shoreline.

Not sure.

Taking the sketch I hold it up next to my screen as I scroll the map. There are a lot of possibilities.

The only way I'm going to figure this out is to do a little field trip.

29

E arly the next morning I'm up and out, my route planned. I haven't used my bike in years, but find it with tires filled, chain oiled, and gears in order. Which can only mean Victor's been keeping it serviced.

I love my step-dad.

With my bike loaded in my Jeep, I begin my route five miles down from Fort Hunt with intentions of going ten total. If I haven't found the location by then, I'll have to regroup.

Dressed in long workout pants and a long sleeve hoodie, I enter the bike path and cruise along. The morning sun shines bright on the Potomac and I thank the weather gods for a nice day. Other bikers zoom by me, but I pay them minimal attention as I study the shoreline.

I stop here and there, climbing off and walking, comparing the surroundings to the sketch.

Minutes tick into hours and still nothing.

Eventually, I take a break and eat a power bar. I've got about a mile left in my game plan. If this doesn't pan out, I might have to loop in Reggie. Which I don't want to do.

I climb back on my bike and about a half mile down, I turn off into a marina.

Slowly, I pull through, circling past old boats up on blocks. Toward the end, I discover a boat rental place, closed for the season. I peddle back the other way spying the casino way across the Potomac and on the other side.

This tiny marina and boatyard sit deserted for the winter, tucked into the shore and hidden in the woods.

Perfect for murder.

Getting off my bike, I take out the sketch and turn a slow circle, comparing the details. Those puzzle pieces click in.

This is the place. I'm sure of it, yet the angle is still a bit off.

Past the boat rental house and across the marsh sits a path in the woods. I climb back on my bike and peddle around to the path. It cuts through the trees, leading further out into the thickets, going all the way to the end until I can't go any further.

And bingo.

This is it. I hold the sketch up. Yes, this it. This is where it occurred forty years ago. And this is where I'll be tonight.

30

I go throughout the rest of my day eager for the events to come, like a kid waiting on Santa.

I take my time getting ready, cross-checking my things, working out the scenarios in my mind. I'll do him right there. I'll hang him by whatever rope he brings.

Perfect justice.

If he's the man I saw standing on top the fort, he's average height and weight. And let's not forget he's sixty something, possibly seventy years old. If I can't take down and kill an old guy, then I don't know what to say.

This isn't the business I should be in.

Dressed in cargo pants and a long sleeve thick black tee, I tuck my usual things down inside the pockets: pepper spray, taser, nylon zip ties, lock picks, duct tape, pocket knife. The full face neoprene mask I slide into my back pocket.

I arrive plenty early, driving my Jeep back into the trees until it's hidden from sight.

When darkness settles in, I climb out and slip the bokken I use in Aikido down its holder strapped to my back.

Through the shadows, I take in the trees and the rough cut path leading to the end where the hanging will occur.

Other than the sound of the casino in the distance, I hear nothing.

Other than the scent of a nearby dead animal, I smell nothing.

Other than the moon shadows flicking through the branches, I see nothing.

Other than the crisp November air, I feel nothing.

Eight o'clock comes. Nine. Ten. By 10:30 doubt and disappointment have settled in. I've miscalculated. Which means somewhere tonight he's going to get away with another murder.

I tune in to myself, waiting for that part of me that recognizes evil nearby, and nothing comes.

My core temp runs hot, but the chill in the air settles into my bones. Not good. I shake out my arms and legs and rotate my neck, warming up.

Reaching through the open driver's window, I take the binoculars from the dash and I step from the trees and across the path. I study the calm water glistening by the lights cast from the distant casino. Across the marsh near the boarded-up boat-rental house, something glints in the darkness.

Squinting my eyes, I stare hard, waiting. And there it is again, a tiny glimmer.

Lifting the binoculars, I zero in on the area, and all the air rushes from my lungs. It's a woman hanging from the dock adjacent to the boathouse.

Shit.

And by the look of her swaying body and bugged eyes, she's already dead.

My teeth grind together. *Dammit.*

My binoculars drift past her, looking for a child, and I spy a boy I'd say is about ten or so propped up in a chair, still unconscious. Good. I'll figure out what to do with him so he doesn't wake up and see her.

Through the night, a motor purrs to life and I swerve the binoculars away from the boy in the direction of the sound. Headlights don't flick on, but a vehicle emerges from between the dry-docked boats.

It's him—the Suicide Killer.

And he has to go right past the entrance to my path on the way out.

I race back over to my Jeep. I hate leaving the boy but this is the only chance I'll have to find out who this killer is. I'll follow the killer back to whatever sewer he crept from, and I'll take him down. He ends tonight.

Like him, I leave my lights off and the engine of my Jeep hums low as I drive down the path with trees lining and covering both sides of me. I round the last curve, right as his car rolls past.

Perfect.

A beige four-door Corolla. Such a nonthreatening vehicle.

I try to get a look at his face, but with the dark interior of the car I make out only an outline.

Allowing him to get several paces ahead, he turns right onto the Parkway and I pull from the path. At this time of night, traffic runs light. He flicks on his lights as his car picks up pace, and I merge to follow.

He travels a few miles, and I pace at a careful distance. Finally, he exits, weaving his way through Alexandria. He goes through a few lights and eventually pulls into the parking lot of a sprawling two-story building.

Across the street from the building sits a medical plaza

and I pull in there. I grab my binoculars and watch as he circles to park in a spot. Turning off his car, he climbs out, and my pulse inches up as I get my first look at the Suicide Killer.

And, yes, it's the same man who was standing on top of the dilapidated fort. Average height, a bit round in the middle, thick flannel jacket, khakis, glasses, and a beanie.

He locks his driver's door and walks up a stone path. As he beeps himself in a side door, he takes off his beanie to show a balding gray head.

I move my binoculars off him and over to the front where a lit up sign sits. It reads AVEDA RETIREMENT LIVING.

The Suicide Killer lives in a retirement home.

What the hell?

Even though the killer beeped himself into the building, I can probably figure a way in too. But that boy back at the marina comes forefront in my brain. It's more important that I go back and make sure he doesn't wake to find his mother hanging in front of him.

From Aveda Retirement Living, I race across town to the small boat yard. But too much time has passed and as I near the entrance, an ambulance cuts past. I'm too late.

That poor kid.

I had no choice, though. Leaving the boy was the only way to track the killer.

And now that I know where he lives, I'm going to figure out who he is.

As soon as I get back to the dorm, I grab my laptop and find a quiet place in the campus library. I bring up a search on Virginia plates and type the Suicide Killer's number in. The site kicks back a name.

Bart Novak.

Next, I type in <Bart Novak: Alexandria, Virginia> and I

get back his current address at Aveda Retirement Living. His birthdate puts him at 64 years old. My search also kicks back a degree in Journalism.

Next, I type in <Bart Novak: Virginia Employment> and I get several hits for travel writing. I click through a few of the sites. I find a friendly photo of him looking proud to the camera with a tiny and professional smile. I zoom in on his green eyes behind thick glasses, searching, but only a welcoming person peers back, no darkness.

Scrolling down I read his bio...lived and traveled all over the states, known for his humorous articles on small town living, award-winning, freelance, enjoys all life has to offer, blah, blah, blah.

Lived all over the States. Killed all over the States. Same thing.

Next, I type in <Bart Novak: Alexandria, Virginia: Current Family> and I get back nothing. No spouse, no children, no grandchildren. He's a loner.

But what about past family? I type in <Bart Novak: Alexandria, Virginia: Family History> and an obituary pops up. I click on it. It appears to be a Vivian Novak. I read, "Survived by one son, Bartholomew Novak."

Bart.

Next, I type in <Vivian Novak: Alexandria, Virginia> and I get a link to a fifty-year-old newspaper article. I click on it and a black and white photo of a woman pops up, not smiling and with long brown hair. "Vivian Novak, age 33, found hanging in an apparent suicide," I read.

Bingo. I keep scanning the article, passing over the irrelevant information and noting key facts. Over the course of a week, she tried to commit suicide three times. The first she slit her wrists. The second she took a handful of pills. And the third and final time she hung herself.

Bled out. Overdose. Hanging.

Bart Novak is recreating his mother's suicide attempts.

I backtrack and read more carefully. "Vivian Novak was found all three times by her son, Bart Novak."

No wonder he's emotionally screwed.

Next, I type in <Vivian Novak: Alexandria, Virginia: Residence Fifty Years Ago> and I get back one hit. I click through and narrow in on the address where the body was found last week with Mom's degraded DNA. The same address where a suicide/murder occurred forty years ago.

So fifty years ago on November 10th, Bart finds his mother bleeding out in their home. A few days later he finds her in their car parked not far away in Fort Hunt with a handful of pills in her stomach. Then two days after that, he finds her hanging over near that boatyard.

Fast forward ten years and he recreates the suicides right in Alexandria where it all began. Except he goes from slit wrists to a slit neck and from a few pills to many. He's making sure the women die.

But he couldn't keep the cycle up in Alexandria and so he moves around—New Orleans, Chicago, Portland, and on and on. His job as a freelance writer allows for that.

So what has brought him back to Alexandria? The 50th anniversary of his mother's death? Maybe, but I'm not sure he would chance dots being connected. No, it might be something else.

So every year in the month of November he does his suicide kills to memorialize his mother. But no one ever makes the connection because they are suicides, not murders. They're never investigated as a homicide. Add to that the fact they are spread out all over the states and it's a perfect scenario.

Yet...where does the kid come in?

Bart found his mother all three times. He's recreating it all. He wants other children to find their mothers too. The question is, how does he get so close to the mother and child to pull all this off? Is it the fact he's a published writer and "trustworthy"?

Every November and no one has connected the dots.

My mother did.

But she couldn't figure out exactly who he was or predict where he would be next.

Or she did and was either cautious of him or she saw him as a worthy adversary. Someone to be studied. Not caught.

Bart won't kill again until November of next year. He's done for now.

This can all be over with as soon as tomorrow. Yet something stops me. Perhaps Bart is the only one who truly knows why Mom's degraded DNA was found. Possibly Bart and my mother knew each other. Maybe she didn't see him as a worthy adversary and was indeed fearful of him.

Going with the fear idea, exactly what about him is so scary?

I mean, other than the fact he's the Suicide Killer.

Sitting back for a second, I close my eyes and I bring up his image as he stepped from his car, a little hunched over, a harmless old man.

A conversation I had with my mom years ago comes back to me.

"Are you ever scared of the killers you hunt?" I ask her.

She pauses, and I get the distinct impression she's weighing her answer carefully. Like she's not quite sure if she should or wants to tell me the truth. Then she blows out a breath and says, "There's only one I've ever truly been wary of and he's never been caught."

It's got to be Bart Novak, and this solidifies my decision. I want to meet him. I want to meet the monster who put such unease into the evil that was my mother.

32

T he following afternoon I arrive at Aveda Retired
Living via public transportation. I walk right up to
the front desk, show my fake student ID, and I tell
the woman working the counter that I'm a student in the
field of social services and would like to volunteer.

And it's that easy. Within thirty minutes, I've filled out an
application, have signed a release form, and am currently in
the game room helping to set up Thanksgiving decorations.

Bart Novak sits over to the right, decorating cookies with
a group of elderly people. He's laughing. They're laughing.
Everyone's talking. Music plays softly in the background.

Just a normal old man, decorating cookies and blending
in.

Paige Akins was the name of the woman I was too late to
save last night. A single woman in her thirties, survived by
one child and an ex-husband. When Bart Novak meets his
final end, I'll list every single name, starting with Paige and
moving backward through the years. He'll know exactly why
he's dying by my hand.

For now, though, the Suicide Killer is done. He's

retreated to the safety of this façade. His defenses are down. It's the perfect time to insert myself into his life.

Climbing down from the step ladder, I take a few fake seconds to admire my decoration expertise of the dancing turkeys dangling from the ceiling. Bart gets up and walks over to the supply table to get more decorations.

Time to "bump" into him.

Done with admiring my work, I cross over to the supply table, too, and pretend to put entirely too much consideration into which decoration I want to work with next—the utensils that need rolling into decorative napkins or the ziplock bag full of fake leaves that get stapled to the bulletin board.

Turning, I smile. "Hi, I'm Maggie Cain. I'm new here."

With a smile of his own, Bart holds out his hand. "Bart Novak, nice to meet you."

I wave my hand around the facility. "Great place."

"It is. Good people." He makes a selection from the supplies—a tube of white icing—and turns to more fully look at me. Like his photo I saw on the writing website, his expression comes across welcoming. "We don't get many volunteers your age," he says.

"I'm new to the area and looking to stay busy. Fresh start and all of that."

"Fresh start?" He chuckles. "You're too young for fresh starts."

I give a small shrug. "I recently suffered a loss and so... there you go."

Behind the thick glasses, his deep-set green eyes take on an honest look of empathy as he reaches out and touches my shoulder in this grandfatherly way that takes me off guard. "I'm sorry to hear that."

"It was my..." I glance away, working up just enough

brave emotion for him to believe. "It was my mother." Closing my eyes, I give myself a second to fake getting my emotions back into control. And when I look into Bart's face again, it's there—the connection I was hoping to establish on this first meet.

He gives my shoulder another gentle squeeze. "Well, you've made a good choice. Throwing yourself into meaningful work makes everything clearer."

Hm, is that how he justifies things? As long as he's giving back, he can perform his yearly ritual of grieving his mother?

Well, that's not interesting at all. That's just warped.

33

On the way back to the dorm, I swing by my home to see how everyone made out on Victor's impromptu trip.

I find Daisy and Justin in the kitchen, laughing and making dinner, and I step in. "How'd it go? Everyone have fun?"

They both glance up—Daisy from mashing potatoes and Justin from slicing tomatoes—and their smiles fade when they see me.

"Fine," Daisy says.

"What she said," echoes Justin.

I look between them, sensing the chill. When did I become the bad guy here? What, because I ratted Justin out to Victor, I'm on the outs? And what's up with Daisy? This can't be about me taking her to see that house. Is she mad at me about Justin, too?

Daisy grinds salt and pepper over the potatoes. "If you're here for dinner, we'll need to figure something out. We didn't make enough."

I get it. Loud and clear. They'd rather I not be here. Fine.

Join the club. Tommy's not talking to me and now neither are my siblings. But at least my brother and sister have to forgive me at some point. It's sort of required—being blood-related and all.

Right?

How is it I can exact justice and experience no regret, but disappointing my family makes me feel like scum?

I glance one last time at Daisy to see her focused across the great room and over to the muted TV. News crews surround the small marina and boatyard where Paige Akins was found hung last night. A ticker tape along the bottom runs details of the apparent suicide.

The TV flicks off and I glance over to see Daisy pointing the remote at it. She's tired of death. I get it. Believe me.

It's going to be okay, I want to tell her. I'm going to bring the person who did this to my kind of justice.

But I don't say anything and instead, turn around and leave. Daisy doesn't want to be part of my world, my obsession. She's making that loud and clear, and I need to respect that.

34

As I stroll down the dormitory hall some thirty minutes later, I hope Sabrina figured out her snoring because I now officially have no place to retreat.

Up ahead and to the right I note our door sits propped open and as I draw near, crying and blubbering filters out. A quick glance in shows Sabrina consoling another student.

Turning around, I walk back the way I came. I barely have a grip on emotions as it is. There's no way I'm inserting myself into that scene right now. I'll say something wrong.

Cutting past the elevator, I shoulder open the exit door, take one flight down, and as I'm rounding to the bottom floor, I run right into Zach.

"Hey." He grins. "What are you doing here?"

"I live here." I point up. "Third floor."

"I didn't realize." He chuckles. "Second floor."

I guess that makes sense with both of us on the signup sheet for campus patrol.

He takes a few steps down. "Thanks again for the other night."

"Oh, sure. That's what friends are for and all that." Friends, yes, that's what we are. I stop him in the stairwell. "You'll tell me the truth, right?"

His dark brows go up. "About?"

"Am I a good listener? Do you feel like you can talk to me?"

Folding his arms, he leans back against the wall. "Yes, you're a listener, but you're not a talker. When it comes to communication it's typically one way with you. And when you do talk, I sense it's filtered."

"Filtered, as in lies?"

"As in carefully formulated."

"That sounds like the politically correct way to say lies."

To that, Zach shrugs. "Okay, then."

"Do you feel as if I keep secrets?" I ask.

"Yes," he answers without pause. "But this isn't new behavior and it certainly shouldn't come as news to you so why are you worried about this now?"

But I don't answer his questions and instead, ask another. "Am I a good person?"

"Yes," he answers, again without pause.

I breathe out, more worried about his response than I realized.

"You hold responsibility for things you shouldn't," he says. "You're scared to make mistakes."

"Good observation."

"Whatever it is that's brought this introspective side of you out, you'll work through it. You always do. I know better than to ask you, so just know you can share with me if you want. You need someone you can trust to talk to. I've always wanted that for you."

Me, too, and honestly I was thinking that might be Daisy.

Hiking his backpack onto his shoulder, he glances at his phone. "Good talk? Because I've got an evening class."

I wave him on. "All good. Thanks."

Zach takes the last few steps down and leaves through the exit door. My brother and sister are home right now laughing and eating dinner, glad I'm not there. And I'm here wanting to be there. They're the whole reason I stayed local.

They want a "normal" sister. Okay, I can be "normal". What would a normal sister do? Cook them dinner? I can cook dinner. I walked in on them laughing. I can laugh. Or I can fake a good laugh.

Bart Novak was laughing with his elderly friends in a warm and intimate way that didn't come across as a show. He came across as having true joy and affection. Then again he's had years to practice and fine-tune the show.

Practice makes perfect?

Maybe it is that simple.

Dare I say I can learn from him? Learn to blend. Mom certainly had the blending thing down pat. She probably learned the technique by observing all the killers she hunted.

Who the hell knows?

Either way, I've got to figure out how to mend whatever fences I've broken with Daisy and Justin. Bart Novak is done killing for now and not an immediate threat. I'll bring him to justice, there is no doubt, but I should focus on my family more.

As I'm pushing through the exit door outside, my phone rings with an incoming call from Reggie.

Thank God. "Hey," I say.

"Hey, so I've got some odd information."

"Hang on." With a glance around, I zip up my jacket and

cut through a clump of kids to find a private spot to talk. "Okay, go ahead."

"That house with your mom's degraded DNA sample has quite the history. There have been three suicides at that house. Fifty years ago, forty years ago, and one last week."

Of course, I already know this, but I wait and listen.

"In addition to finding your mom's degraded DNA, the team found one single strand of long brown hair that they've approximated is fifty years old and matched as female. They found an identical strand of hair in the car a few days later where another suicide occurred."

In the picture I saw online, Bart's mother had long brown hair. Interesting. I'd lay a solid wager they're going to find another strand on the hanging victim. "And my mom's degraded DNA?"

"I don't know. I still can't figure out what put her in that house. I'm not giving up, though. But I thought you'd find that hair thing interesting."

"I do, thanks."

"I tried digging into the suicides forty and fifty years ago at that house, but evidence collection was done completely different and I didn't find anything. If there is anything to find its probably sitting in a box in a dusty police warehouse."

"Yeah, probably. But the facts are, years ago a team showed up on the scene, saw a suicide, and called it a day. There was nothing to collect because no crime occurred."

Reggie says, "You and I both know something fishy is going on. I also did some digging to see if they got a DNA match on the hair strand, but nothing is there."

And nothing will be there. Bart Novak's mother won't be in a police database. Bart Novak won't either. He's squeaky clean. He hides the real him from everyone except his victims. The investigators will be on a wild goose chase. There's no way they'll match anything to Bart. He's too well hidden.

But I really don't want Reggie digging in and finding Bart. "If you could just focus on that degraded DNA and what put Mom in that house that would be great."

"For sure. Like I said, just wanted you to know what I had found so far."

"Appreciate it."

We hang up, and I stand outside the dorm, thinking through things.

Bart is paying his respects by leaving a strand of his mother's hair on the victims. It's his ritual. But has he done it over the years? I don't know. Likely not.

To me, a strand of foreign hair would link everything together. Unless he hid the hair at the scene or went back to leave it afterward. He sure didn't hide anything this time, though.

But this time was different. It was the 50th anniversary of this mother's death.

Or...he's hoping connections will be made. He's done with his kills and he wants to be found.

I don't know. A successful serial killer who wants to be caught? Something's off.

Bart found his mother hanging at the old marina. And somewhere along the way, he kept a portion, if not all, of her hair.

Which means, he has it.

Somewhere in Aveda Retirement, Bart Novak has strands of his dead mother's hair. He keeps her with him all the time.

And I'm going to find it.

35

The following afternoon I sign in as Maggie Cain at the Retirement Home and ask the desk clerk, "Any idea where Bart Novak is? I met him yesterday and would love to say hi."

The clerk's face lights up. "I adore Mr. Novak. Everyone around here does." She holds out her hand. "Holleen, nice to meet you."

"You, too." So everyone around here adores ole Bart, huh? That's not something someone would say about me, but Bart, he's out there—all open, friendly, and generous.

"Maggie Cain," Bart's voice comes from behind and I turn to see him crossing the lobby to where I stand.

"You remember me?"

"I never forget a pretty face with a keen mind."

I'm not sure anyone has ever described me like that, but I go with it. "I was just asking Holleen here where you were. I wanted to say hi."

"That's very kind of you. I was just heading to reading hour."

"Reading hour?"

Holleen says, "Once a week a preschool group comes and several of the residents take turns reading to them. Today is Bart's turn."

Bart winks at Holleen. "It's the reason we're all here. To give back."

It's not why I'm here.

He nods across the lobby toward a cozy outdoor area with cushioned wicker chairs and warmers intermittently placed. A group of kids and elderly people sit waiting, everyone clumped under blankets and some sipping warm drinks.

I follow Bart out and he motions me to sit on a bench next to a woman dressed in scrubs, presumably a nurse. While I do he makes his way through the crowd of kids, leaning down here and there to touch their little heads.

"How long have you all being doing this?" I ask the nurse.

"Oh, just since Bart moved in about a year ago. It was his idea and everyone really took to it."

Shifting, I tuck my hands into my jacket pockets. "This is my second day. Everyone seems so close and happy."

"We are. It's a great place to work and live."

Bart nods at an elderly lady as he picks up the book he's supposed to read. Polite. Well adjusted. Liked. Admired. Loved. This man is not meeting my expectations.

"It's nice that you're here," the nurse says. "We don't get a lot of kids your age who want to volunteer."

"Just looking to give back, that's all."

Bart makes himself comfortable under a blanket, taking a second to clean his glasses. Holleen comes through the patio door and over to me, motioning me to scoot to the middle of the bench.

Between the nurse on one side and Holleen on the other,

it's a bit too close for my comfort level. But it would look entirely too odd if I got up now before story time. Instead, I cross my legs, tuck my hands further in, and try to make myself a tiny bit of space.

"Just one big happy family," I say.

The nurse chuckles. "That it is."

"Bart's a real special guy."

"He is. We really lucked out when he moved in here. He keeps things energetic and fills the place with love. He's everyone's father, brother, grandfather. He fills a lot of voids."

Bart Novak, man of the year.

Leaning over, Holleen shushes us. "Storytime is starting and Mr. Novak doesn't like it when we talk."

36

L ike me, Bart Novak has been shaped by a history involving our mothers. We both have a family we love, albeit his is one he created at Aveda. He cares for those he holds dear.

Unlike me, he has an extroverted personality. Was he always that way? Does he have some gene I don't? My mother was extroverted too. A learned behavior among serial killers? I don't know.

I try to envision myself being extroverted—smiling, making jokes, woman of the hour—and I almost laugh. My family would think I was high.

Downshifting, I pull into our neighborhood, winding back through the homes, and I parallel park along the street. I note Mom's Lexus that now belongs to Daisy parked a few spots up. A quick peek into the garage shows Victor's home, too.

When I walk inside, Victor lays sprawled on the couch with Justin beside him, sharing a bowl of BBQ chips, drinking root beer, and watching hockey. Usually, Victor is in his office working. I'm sure this father-son time is a direct result of the recent issues with Justin. I'm glad Victor is conscientious of spending time with Justin, but I'm also very curious if he knows anything more about the degraded DNA.

"Hey," I say.

Victor glances up but I don't get the usual smile from him. What, now he's mad at me too? What the hell is going on with my family?

I focus on Justin instead. "Whatever happened to football?" I ask.

My brother shrugs. "Not my thing."

"Where's Daisy?" I look around.

"In the basement looking through Mom's stuff," Victor says.

What?

I don't say anything else and instead, take the stairs straight down. I step into the basement to find Daisy sitting on the carpet with all of Mom's boxes open and spread out.

She looks up. "I've been going through everything of Mom's and stuff is missing."

Yeah, because I took it. "Like what?"

"She was organized, everything dated. But some of these files skip dates like papers are gone." Daisy points. "Here she references a journal, but where's the journal?"

"Why are you so wrapped up in Mom? I've told you everything I know."

"And I want to know more," Daisy snaps, and it takes me off guard. "What's wrong with that?"

I sigh. "Dad knows you're down here."

"Yes, I told him. I also told him that you overheard him on the phone and about the degraded DNA from Mom. I told him we drove to that house in Alexandria."

"You did *what*? That was between you and me." It also explains why I just got the cold shoulder from Victor.

"I'm not keeping secrets from Dad. Why should I?"

"You didn't tell him about Mom's affair—"

Victor clears his throat, and I spin around to see him standing on the bottom step. *Shit.*

We freeze in place. I don't say anything. Neither does Daisy.

His jar hardens. "What affair?"

I take a breath, my brain spinning with half-truths. But the half-truths, the outright lies, the secrets—those are what has brought us to this moment. It's why my family is mad at me. Everything I do and say to my family has the best intentions. But sometimes it's time to speak the truth and know that people are about to get hurt.

Daisy opens her mouth to talk and I stop her. "Let me." I turn back to Victor. "Mom had a locker at the Dunn Loring Station. I found a key and I went to retrieve the items. It was a box full of letters, some between Mom and Marji, and others between Mom and my real dad, Seth. Love letters. Some dated fairly recently. There were also photos of them, some old and others new." Of course, I leave out the gruesome details of those photos.

Victor's jaw tightens more, his muscles popping, but I have to push through. I have to tell him the rest. I swallow. "I also found a paternity test that proves Daisy is my full sister. Genetically, she is Seth's daughter too."

"Where is this box?" he demands.

"I was mad and burned it at Patch and Paw in the crematorium."

With a sigh, he runs his fingers through his thick black and gray hair. "I knew it. Goddamn it, I knew it. I knew she was seeing Seth."

My eyes widen. That was not the response I was expecting. I was expecting shock, not anger. I glance over to Daisy to see tears gathered in her eyes. Tears for Victor.

"You're my dad," she whispers.

"Of course I am." He looks between us. "You are both *my* daughters. Not Seth's. *Mine.*"

My throat rolls with a raw swallow. I'm so grateful and lucky this man raised me. "Dad, I'm sorry I didn't tell you about overhearing you on the phone. I guess I thought you'd come to us when you knew something. I don't know. I shouldn't have gone to Daisy behind your back. I'm sorry."

His hazel eyes move between us and they take on a loving, but firm look. "You listen to me. I will not have my daughters lying to me. We will be a family of no secrets. Do you hear me?"

No secrets but the biggest of all. Mom was a serial killer and I ended her life.

But instead, I nod.

"As soon as I know something about the degraded sample, I will tell you." He looks between us again. "I love both of my girls very much."

"Love you, too," we echo.

He turns then, giving us his back, and he walks back up the steps.

When he's all the way upstairs, I look at my sister sitting in the pile of Mom's stuff and my heart sinks. I wanted to share this with Daisy, but now I don't. "I'm sorry. I didn't mean to drag you into anything or make you feel like you had to keep secrets. I'm so sorry."

With a sniff, she wipes her eyes. "We're good." She closes a folder and slides it back into a box. "Dad said there were a lot of things in here that Mom was obsessed with. I guess killers she couldn't catch."

Or killers she wanted to study.

Daisy waves her hand over Mom's stuff. "All these notes on murders. It's enough to drive someone crazy. I can't believe she did this for a living."

Going with the honesty trend, I say, "You're right, stuff is missing. I took it."

"I figured as much." Her lips twitch. "A little light reading?"

I chuckle. "Something like that."

We're silent and then she says, "Do you think you can just let all of this go? Do you think you can find another hobby that doesn't involve tracking serial killers?"

"What, like doing my nails and straightening my hair?"

"No." Daisy laughs. "Guess not."

"If you want to see the things I took, just ask. I'm happy to show."

But she doesn't answer and instead pulls over another box and lifts off the lid. She's more interested than she wants to admit. But I won't push. I'll let her come to me.

37

I 'm going to lose my family if I don't continue being honest and sharing. It's not enough to be present. I have to communicate, and while it doesn't have to be all honesty all the time, it does have to contain some meaningful truth.

Like what happened last night in the basement with Victor and Daisy.

Bart Novak has his own version of meaningful truth. He keeps the memory of the person he loved most in this world close, even decades after her death. He found his mother bleeding out. He found her in a car with a belly full of pills. He found her hanging from a tree. He wasn't able to save her that final time. He lost her and now he's recreating her suicide attempts year after year after year.

Yes, it's his own version of meaningful truth.

I watched my mother in the kill room. My real father, too. I saw pictures of them taking delight in mutilating people.

Now I take delight in doing the same, though my victims deserve it.

Is that my own version of meaningful truth? Yes, it must be.

Me and Bart, we both have our skeletons. And everyone knows skeletons hide in closets. Where is your closet, Bart? Where are you hiding your trophies? Where are you hiding your mother's hair?

I bet I know where.

. . .

"Hi," I greet Holleen, the desk clerk, just like I've done every time I come here to volunteer at Aveda Retirement.

"Hi!" She grins, eyeing the tin of cookies that I brought. "Whatcha got there?"

"A little present for Mr. Novak." I glance at her computer. "Mind telling me which room he's in?"

"Oh, sure. I don't need to look it up. He's on the second floor in the studio apartment wing in room 204."

Opening the tin, I hand her a white chocolate macadamia nut one. "Homemade and for you." Homemade at the bakery, but I digress.

"Aren't you sweet?" She holds up a hand. "But no thank you. Once I hit my forties, any bite of sugar or butter goes straight to my butt. And lord knows I don't need another dimple there."

Too much information, but okay. I put the cookie back in the tin, and I make my way over to the elevator.

It's two in the afternoon and according to the schedule I glanced at the last time I was here, Bart is leading a Tai Chi class. I've timed this perfectly, factoring in enough time to snoop, leave the cookie tin with a note, and then get "caught" by a returning Bart.

I'm very interested to see his reaction to my invasion of his personal space.

As I make my way to room 204, I give a nod to one resident, stop and say hi to another, wave hello to the nurse.

I round the corner to Bart's room, already digging in my pocket for my lock picks.

No one is around and it only takes me a few seconds to get inside. I leave the door cracked open, wanting Bart to see it and to know someone is in here before he enters.

His room looks much like a small hotel suite with a queen size bed, a dresser and TV, a desk and chair, a small couch, a bathroom, one single closet, and a tiny kitchenette.

As expected, it's neat, tidy, and clean with sparse decorations. There's a framed watercolor painting on each wall—all nature scenes—a waterfall, the woods, a frozen lake. In the bottom corner, Bart has signed each one. Not bad, Bart. He's a decent artist.

Putting the tin down on the small dark wood desk, I wander over the nightstand and pick up a silver-framed, black and white photo of his mother. Though her lips hold a pleasant curve, her eyes appear sad and the emotion I sense there moves through me.

I set the photo back down and look under Bart's bed to find one single pair of men's slippers.

Next, I slide open each drawer in his dresser and find neatly folded underwear, t-shirts, sweat pants, and various other things. I sift through them, but he's got nothing tucked down hiding.

His desk comes after that where I note a framed degree from an online university, a B.S. in Journalism. Beside that sits a closed laptop.

I open each drawer of his desk to find neatly organized office supplies.

When I turn to head to the closet I spy a wooden cane in the corner and I zero in on the unique walking stick medallions nailed into the cane. I pick the cane up, slowly rotating it, studying the metal decorations.

Son of a bitch, it's his trophies right here out in the open. One collectible medallion from each city where he's killed, to include two from right here in Alexandria.

But where would he be keeping his mother's hair?

A quick search of his closet shows it just like the rest, clean and organized. Perhaps he keeps it in his car. If so, that'll have to be for another day.

I close his closet, crossing back over to the tin of cookies. A brief glance of my watch shows he should be returning any second. Good. I take a yellow sticky note off his desk and write a quick *Thank you for being so welcoming. Homemade macadamia. I hope you like them!*

As I smooth the note on the tin, I catch sight of one single throw pillow on his couch. A throw pillow is not unusual, but this one is. Pink and white with lace trim, it looks every bit as old as it is. I recognize this pillow.

I glance back over to the framed photo of his mother where she sits proper and straight on the edge of an antique chair with the same throw pillow wedged in the corner behind her.

Bart kept this pillow for a reason and I don't waste a second as I pick it up and inspect it. I rotate it slowly, studying the hand-sewn work. I examine the seams finding three sides sewn and one with a zipper.

I open the delicate zipper to the white stuffing inside. I move it around, tunneling my hand down and in, and my fingers snag on plastic. Stepping closer to the window, I open the pillow a bit more and peer down in, and sure enough, it's long brown human hair encased in airtight plastic.

His mom's hair.

More secrets out right in the open and not hidden under lock and key. Hiding in plain sight. I'm the one who lurks. Not him.

What kind of son keeps his dead mother's hair in a pillow?

What kind of daughter keeps her dead mother's serial killer files?

I zip the pillow up and I'm about to place it back on the couch when the door creaks open.

Here we go.

With the pillow behind me, I turn to see Bart standing in the open door, dressed in blue sweatpants from his recent Tai Chi. His thick glasses sit propped on the tip of his nose.

Pushing those glasses up, he slides his flip flops off and places them to the side, looking pointedly at my running shoes. "No shoes allowed."

I find it odd this is the first thing he says to me. "Oh, sorry." I nod to the desk and the tin of cookies. "I brought you some homemade treats. Your door was cracked open. I knocked and when no one answered, I came on in. I hope that was okay."

He knows I'm lying. He knows he didn't leave his door unlocked.

He steps further into the room. "Of course."

Hiding in plain sight. But what I have tucked behind my back is his weak spot. Let's see what happens when it's exposed. I bring the pillow out from behind. "This is beautiful. I was just admiring the stitch work."

One second he's over by the door and the next he's right in front of me, moving quicker than any old man I've ever seen. He yanks the pillow from my hands. "That belonged to my mother. Don't touch it!"

Holding my hands up, I make sure my eyes take on a look of remorse and fear as I stare into his angry green eyes. "I'm sorry. I didn't know. I was just bringing you cookies. I'm sorry."

His jaw vibrates, his breathing rasps. He closes his eyes and when next he opens them, he's back to friendly and approachable Bart Novak.

"Forgive me," he says. "I didn't mean to scare you."

I take a step toward the door. "It's okay. I get it. It belonged to your mom. I get that way with my mom's stuff, too. Memories."

He nods as he gently puts the pillow back, taking extra care to situate it just so. "It's been a long time but it's very painful for me."

"I understand. But maybe you should store the pillow in a safe place versus out in the open like this. Aren't you worried about it getting damaged?"

"No. Mother will always be with me. Everywhere I go."

I look at the pillow. "I'm not sure I'll ever get to that point of wanting my mother near."

Bart circles his room, his gaze touching on the cane, the photo of his mother, the dresser, the tin of cookies. Don't worry, I made sure everything is in its place.

He says, "I used to push people away because of my past. I even lost a woman I loved and wanted to marry. But I changed. I realized I needed to open up and now I have an abundance of friends who care deeply for me. They are my family. They saved me."

His words ring deep and true and I simply stand in his small studio and digest them.

Bart opens the tin and selects a cookie. He takes a bite,

smiling. "Delicious." He walks me over to the door. "Will I see you around?"

"Oh, yes."

"Good. And, Maggie, please don't ever step foot in my apartment unless I'm here." He closes the door in my face and the resounding click of his lock echoes in the hall.

38

From Aveda Retirement I go straight to Tommy's place. It's been days since I've seen him last and assuming his schedule is the same, he should be home.

I park my Jeep along the curb where I normally do, cross behind the house owned by the young family he rents from, and walk the back path to the front door of his "cottage". One day I'm sure this place will be occupied by an aging parent of the couple who owns the house, but for now, it belongs to Tommy.

I spy his bike, kickstand down, propped on the concrete slab next to his studio apartment. An unexpected spike of nerves moves through me. I'd like to think I'm indifferent to what people think, but the truth is, I'm not.

Actually, I should rephrase. I'm not indifferent to Tommy, my family, Zach. But my roommate, Sabrina? I don't know, she's kind of working on me. The students in my classes? Not my problem. The people at Patch and Paw? Eh, Dr. O'neal is kind of working on me, too. She's turned a corner in my brain.

Raising my hand, I knock, and my heart surprisingly picks up pace as I wait. There's shuffling from within and then the door swings wide. There stands Tommy—all tall and blonde and beyond desirable.

I clear my throat. "Hi."

He inhales. Exhales. "Hi."

"I want to be with you," I say, always getting right to the point.

"And I want to let you in," he responds. "But honestly, I don't know how."

Okay, wow. That sounds like more of something I would say.

He breathes out again. "I mean, I've never really learned."

For that matter, neither have I.

"Or rather right as I was learning to be a man, everything happened. My sister was murdered by The Decapitator. My parents closed off. And I was left...grieving."

Tommy's older sister was my mother, The Decapitator's, last victim. Of course, Tommy believes, as does everyone else, that The Decapitator was my uncle on my father's side. Tommy and I met in a grieving group for family of murdered victims. Imagine our surprise when we realized his sister was murdered by my "uncle".

"I don't either," I say. "When I was just a little girl I saw The Decapitator cut up a victim." This is a true statement and something only Tommy knows. "That one single event has shaped who I am today. It's quite a history. And now my mother is dead and the more I dig into her past, the more I realize she isn't pristine. But I want to change."

Tommy shifts, propping his shoulder in the door. "Can I ask you a question and require complete honesty?"

"I'll try, Tommy, I promise."

"Are you afraid of *anything?*"

"Yes."

"What?"

"My past. Abandonment. People seeing the real me."

He nods. "Okay, and what do you think will happen, that you'll be alone?"

"Yes," I answer without hesitation. "Absolutely. I don't want to be alone." I pull in a quiet breath. Wow, it's true. For all my desire of "me" time, I don't really want to be alone. I want to have "people", whatever that means. Family. Friends. Loved ones.

With a sigh, Tommy reaches out and grasps my wrist, and as he pulls me in he says, "Then you should know I'm with you because I want to get to know the real you. That's it. It's that simple. All I want is the truth."

I step forward into his apartment and he closes the door. "I need space, yes, but I need you, too. Zach coming back is just that. He's back. I was with him the other night because he went back to that house where The Decapitator held him ready to kill. The same house where my mother was killed." Or rather I killed her. "I'm glad I went because he needed support. I was there as support."

Tommy loops his fingers into my front belt loop and pulls me in. "I understand you're trying to be a good friend. I understand, too, that you need space to be you. I need space, too, as you know. Now that you are privy to my BDAP alter ego. I needed an out, and I found it there."

I don't ask him what happened to that pedophile social worker, I honestly could care less. I like Tommy and I totally understand this side of him. I like even more this honesty trend we have going and so I continue to share. "Daisy and I recently discovered Mom was having an ongoing affair with

Seth, my real father. We also discovered that Daisy is Seth's real daughter, too."

Tommy's expression shifts, going from all things me and him to my family. "Oh my God, does Victor know?"

"Yes, we all had a talk about it. Daisy was crying. Victor was crushed. It was bad."

Tommy pulls me in even more and my arms loop around his sides to clasp at his lower back. "And you?" he asks.

I inhale, soaking in his welcoming leather and soap scent. God, I missed him. "It's a lot. And now there's even a degraded DNA sample of my mother that has shown up in Alexandria at the scene of a suicide."

I stop. Holy shit. I didn't mean to wrangle him into that, too.

"It's okay," he assures me as if reading my mind. "Honesty. That's all I want from you."

I take another breath, unable to grasp what I'm about to share. "Mom spent her life tracking killers, and there was this one she never caught. He's connected to a string of suicide style murders that stretch over forty years. I think the degraded DNA sample comes from this. I'm not entirely sure, but she may have seen this killer when she was just a little girl and it shaped her into who she became—the FBI Director who hunted killers. That maniac is still out there."

His name is Bart Novak and I can get to him.

"Did you talk to Victor about this?"

"No, not yet. He knows about the degraded DNA sample but honestly, I'm not entirely sure about the rest. I'm going off of random notes that I found in one of her files and my own thoughts. I'm not sure she was fully connecting the dots either."

Tommy strokes a warm finger along the outline of my

ear, stopping to caress my lobe. "Probably best to let Victor come to you when he knows more. It sounds like he's dealing with a lot right now given the information on Daisy's real father and your mom's affair."

"My thoughts exactly." I step further into his embrace and nuzzle my lips along his throat. Evil genetic ooze crawls in my veins, but somewhere along the way, I became my own. And now I'm figuring out what all of that means.

For now, it means Tommy and Daisy, Justin and Victor. I'm a sister, daughter, girlfriend, friend. Yet there's a void there that I sense will always be. A void filled only when I embrace that genetic ooze.

Tommy shifts, dipping his lips to fully meet mine. The kiss that follows comes slow and full of promise, not all the fast and furious, raw and gritty we tend to do.

I freefall into it, relishing the slow pace, and I allow myself to be here, right now, with this man.

Undressing each other.

Linking fingers.

Walking naked to the bed.

Making love...

Those are two words I never thought I'd think or say. "Sex" and "intercourse" are more my type of words, but "making love" is the only phrase to describe the tender interaction between us.

Sometimes there are moments that are perfectly still. Almost as if time freezes in a calm and peaceful place. This is one of those moments.

The only downside is that those moments pass too quickly and reality returns.

It always returns.

39

The next morning Sabrina lays sprawled on the bottom bunk furiously typing away on her phone. Her ever-present opera music plays softly in the background, and as I move around the room getting ready for morning classes, it occurs to me that she didn't snore last night.

Or maybe I was so tired I slept right through it.

With an agitated sigh, she tosses her phone down.

It's not like me to get involved, but she did cover for Justin and so I say, "What's wrong?"

With another sigh, she rubs her eyes. "My family. They're taking over my life."

First Tommy sounds like me and now Sabrina. "Maybe if you got better ringtones they wouldn't be so annoying."

She snorts. "Not likely. I thought moving hundreds of miles away would cut the cord, you know? How do you do it? Your family is right here, and they don't consume you." She stops rubbing her eyes and rolls her head to look at me.

"It's more about activity. Every person in my family is busy with their own thing. We all have interests that don't involve the family. It keeps us busy." So busy, in fact, that I lost track of Justin, and Daisy is doing things like calling Mom's old boyfriends.

Sabrina gives some consideration. "I thought the miles between us would give me space to do what I want, but I spend most days on the phone solving their problems. It's exactly what I was doing before and why I wanted away so much."

"Interests." With a nod, she swings her legs over the bed. "That's a fabulous idea. I'm going to find things for them to do so they don't bug me."

And while Sabrina is wanting to cut the familial cord, I'm wanting to reattach it. Interesting how things change.

"Well anyway..." Sabrina picks up her phone, glances at it, and puts it right back down. "Thought I'd better give you a heads up about something."

"And that would be?"

"You know my friend, Erna?"

Not really, but I nod anyway.

"She was in here a few days ago really upset."

That must have been the sobbing I heard coming from the room.

"There are naked and incredibly crude pictures of her circulating the campus and she has no recollection of them being taken. She thinks maybe she was drugged or something. Like Rohypnol, I guess."

I straighten up. "She doesn't remember where she was?"

"She was at that bar over by the used bookstore. You know the one with the blues bands and the picnic style tables, Wish You Were Beer Bar?"

Stupid name, but I nod.

"That's the last thing she remembers. She was talking to one of her professors, doesn't remember anything after that, and then woke up in her car fully clothed." Sabrina picks her phone up again, slides her finger across, and shows me the screen.

I recognize her now. Erna, a Swiss exchange student. Tall and pretty with olive skin and light brown hair. I've seen her around campus and here in the dorm, too. Always smiling and laughing, a happy girl. In this naked picture, though, she's clearly drugged.

Sabrina swipes the screen to show me another photo taken from behind with her propped and posed in a vulnerable and beyond exposed position. My blood boils. "Did she report this?"

"Yes, and campus IT worked at getting them taken down, but this photo went out wide and so many people have seen it. Apparently, this has happened before, too, with other girls. Erna is humiliated and has decided to go back home." My roommate puts her phone back down. "All to say, please be careful out there."

"Oh, I will." I'm finding the son of a bitch who did this and taking him down. "Who is the professor, by the way— the one who she remembers talking to?"

"Professor Kane Gregg, but he's well known around here and liked. He didn't have anything to do with this. It's probably one of the frat guys."

"Hm," I simply say.

40

P rofessor Kane Gregg, thirty-nine years old, six feet tall, sandy brown hair, brown eyes, a competitive cyclist, unmarried, no kids, lives alone in a condo a few blocks from campus. Well-loved by students. Heads up the clean campus initiative. Was an Associate Professor for five years and has been a tenured professor for the same.

Six years ago there was a rumor he was seeing a student but other than that, the man "appears" clean.

Appears being the operative word.

Compared to the Suicide Killer, this guy is a chump, but Bart Novak can wait. He isn't going anywhere. Until next November, his killing is over. He's not an immediate threat. I can't say the same for the professor. He could target another victim as soon as tonight.

Yes, Professor Kane Gregg deserves my focus.

I sit in my Jeep eyeing people as they move in and out of Wish You Were Beer Bar. This is the last thing Erna remembers before waking up disoriented only to find naked pictures of her all over the internet.

According to my digging, Professor Kane Gregg comes

here almost every night, though he hasn't made an appearance yet.

My phone buzzes with a text and my first inclination is to ignore it, but after what happened the last time I did that with Victor and the heart attack, I pick it up and look at it.

Daisy: DAD DOESN'T KNOW MARJI IS MOM'S SISTER, DOES HE?

Me: NO. HE THINKS THEY WERE CHILDHOOD FRIENDS.

Daisy: WHAT THE HELL, LANE? WHY DID MOM HAVE SO MANY SECRETS?

Me: I DON'T KNOW...

Daisy: SHOULD WE TELL HIM?

I want to say no but with all the lies and secrets I type: YOU DECIDE AND I'LL BACK YOU UP.

Daisy: YOU SAID YOU TRACKED MARJI TO RICHMOND AND THAT SHE HAD MOVED. WHAT WAS MARJI'S LAST NAME?

It's only a matter of time before Daisy finds out. Pointing her in the wrong direction is my first inclination, but with a deep breath, I type the truth: MARJOREAM VEGA.

I have officially opened Pandora's box. Anybody can type that name into a search engine and read that she was found stabbed in the woods next to that horrible trailer with the cage, the kidnapped young woman, the torturing devices, and the photos of her kills.

But no one but Daisy and I knows our mother was Marji's sister.

Marji leads to Mom, leads to Seth, leads to their killing spree. It's one big disgusting circle that then leads back to me.

They say cycles can be broken and I fully intend on permanently severing this one.

rofessor Kane Gregg never showed at the bar. I did a drive-by of his condo and sat for a bit watching him watch TV through his open living room blinds. And when he got up to get undressed for bed, I finally called it a night.

The next morning, classes come and go. I do a shift at Patch and Paw, and as I arrive to volunteer at Aveda Retirement, Bart Novak is on his way out.

I jog over to him. "Hello, Mr. Novak, heading out?"

"It's Bart," he grumbles, barely looking at me as he buttons up his thick flannel jacket and continues walking across the parking lot.

Interesting mood. Where's the jovial man I've seen so many times now?

He comes to a stop at a truck with Aveda Retirement Living painted on the doors. In the back lays an ax, a chainsaw, and rope. Well, now, where are you going with those supplies, Bart Novak?

"Heading out?" I ask all innocent curiosity.

"Yes." He opens the driver's door and steps up in.

"It looks like you're doing Aveda business. I'm happy to help."

He nods me to get in. "Fine."

With a little skip around the front of the truck, I climb up in. He cranks the engine followed by the heat and pulls away.

Bart Novak doesn't say a word and so neither do I. He's in a mood. And I'm just curious enough to see why.

At a red light, I glance over to see the driver in the car beside us give me a cursory look. I nod. Don't mind us, folks, we're just two killers, sitting side-by-side in a truck, heading out of the city and into the country to do God knows what.

But honestly, I wouldn't want to be any other place right now.

He exits off the highway and bumps his way over a dirt road, weaving through trees and eventually coming to a stop. He cuts the engine and climbs out. I follow.

Lowering the tailgate of the truck, he points to the chainsaw. "Ever used one?"

"No."

"Heavy and difficult to manipulate, but sometimes a necessity."

Is he giving me a lesson in murder weapons? I don't think so. To my knowledge, he's never used a chainsaw on a victim.

He picks it up, nods for me to take the ax, and disappears through the trees. This is a bit too into the woods for me, but I go with it.

I heft the ax over my shoulder. "So what are we doing? Cutting down a tree?"

"Yes." He stops at a small pine tree, giving it a good study.

"Isn't early to be decorating? Thanksgiving isn't even over yet."

"My mother decorated in November and so I do, too." Done talking, he cranks the chainsaw.

It whirls, then dies.

He cranks it again.

It whirls, then dies.

He cranks it again.

It whirls, then dies.

"Goddamn it!" Bart yells, throwing the chainsaw down. He spins on me so fast that I freeze. But he just grabs the ax from my hands, turns back, and violently assaults the small tree trunk.

Not for the first time, his quick movement has thrown me off. Something tells me Bart's trained in more than Tai Chi.

I've never cut down a tree, but it doesn't look too difficult, especially one that small. "Want me to help?"

"No," he grunts, whacking at the trunk.

For an old man, he is really attacking that thing. "Will you decorate your room with this?"

"No." Whack. Whack.

"Small for the lobby," I note.

Whack. Whack. "This is one of three."

"Why not just buy them from a lot?"

"Because this is better." Whack. Whack.

The small tree falls, and Bart moves onto another.

"Three trees, huh? What, you decorate them Christmas past, present, and future?"

Whack. Whack. "Yes."

"Sure you don't want me to do one?"

"No." Whack. Whack.

"Mr. Novak, you're a bit off today."

Whack. Whack. "It's. Bart."

A few more hard chops, and the second small tree falls. While he starts in on the third one, I grab the first one and drag it over to the truck. I hoist it up and in, listening to his furious chops echoing through the trees.

I go back for the second one, glancing over at Bart's back as he bends over to get a good angle. I can easily take him out. He'll be exhausted after all of this. He won't see me coming. I can knock him unconscious, take the rope he brought, and string him up from a tree.

Death by hanging. Just like his final victims.

Justice.

Instead, I slide the second tree into the truck and as I step through the woods back toward Bart and the third tree, his chopping has subsided. Through the leaves and branches, he kneels beside the third fallen tree, his back hunched over. The sound of soft sobs filter over to me.

What the hell?

Quietly I walk toward him and he glances up. The tears streaming down his cheeks stop me cold.

"I didn't mean to kill it," he quietly says.

It's then I notice a crushed squirrel under the tree. Oh, no.

"It was an accident," he whispers, his voice so quiet I barely hear him.

"Of course it was."

He sniffs. "Is it dead? I don't want it to suffer."

Kneeling down beside him, I give the squirrel a good long study. "Yes, it's dead." This man has spent decades killing innocent women and he sobs over a squirrel? I don't get it.

But the truth is, I would be just as upset, too. Dead

humans are one thing, but dead animals? They're just so innocent.

The ax lays in the pine needles where he must have dropped it. Yes, pick it up and end this killer's life. Right now.

But somehow I find myself helping him to his feet. Assisting him in burying a little squirrel. Securing all three trees with the rope I should have hung him with. Taking the keys from him. And driving him back to Aveda.

I'm not sure what is going on with me, but Bart Novak has nestled in and I can't bring myself to kill him.

At least not yet.

42

When I get back to the dorm, I find Sabrina sitting in the middle of our room on the striped throw rug. Photos spread out around her of various girls all in compromising positions just like Erna.

Sabrina glances up at me. "This is bigger than I thought." She motions to a photo of a redhead girl. "From Argentina." She points to a photo of dark-haired girl. "Spain." A blonde. "Australia." She points to another. "Germany." And another. "Mexico."

Squatting down, I give them all a glance. "Easier to pick on the exchange students. Once they've been photographed and dispersed, the families are less likely to follow up. Like Erna, they want their daughter home."

Sabrina nods. "Yes. I did some follow up with our campus police and they've done some queries, but unless the families are pushing, it falls through the cracks."

Yeah, well, it's not falling through mine.

Picking up a photo of the blonde, I study the surroundings. It looks like the inside of a garage. Professor Kane

Gregg's condo comes with a garage. "Not to sound un-empathetic, but why do you care so much about these girls that you don't even know?"

My roommate picks the photos back up. "Because this happened to me in high school. I was at a party and someone drugged my drink. I woke up naked and violated. It was horrible."

Reaching out, I take her hand, and it's only after I'm squeezing her fingers that I realize I'm touching her. I'm consoling her. It's not something I do on instinct and I love that I am. "This son of a bitch will be found and he will pay for what he's done."

She lifts dark brown eyes to mine and she doesn't say a word, but she believes me.

43

That night I'm sitting in the parking lot of Wish You Were Beer Bar with Professor Kane Gregg inside. I followed him from his condo, and since he just got here, I'll have hours to do a bit of recon.

I backtrack to his condo and park along the street. Through the shadows, I cross over the grounds and come to his building. His condo sits on the second floor with the garage directly underneath. He pulls in and probably walks an interior stairwell up to his condo.

Perfect.

This particular building houses the smaller units typically owned by single people—professionals or retired individuals. Being nine at night and a weekday, most of the occupants are in for the night.

Unless they're out trolling for innocent girls.

Other than a few interior lights of other units, there is no movement and so I don't bother disguising myself as I walk up the few steps that lead to his front door. It's a standard lock and deadbolt and with my lock picks I gain entry.

Professor Kane Gregg has left a few interior lights on

dim, and I use them to navigate by. As expected, he lives in a small one-bedroom condo. Not as expected, the place is a mess. Unmade bed, dishes in the sink, piles of unfolded laundry, a bathroom in dire need of cleaning, and dust covering everything.

For such a good looking and well-dressed man, he keeps a disgusting home.

I don't bother searching his place for evidence of the photos. Frankly, it would take me too long to sift through the mess.

Instead, I head straight down to his garage.

And bingo.

Over in the corner sits the mattress in all the photos and covered in red silk sheets. Black silk sheets drape the wall behind it. Quite the boudoir.

A large spotlight sits beside the mattress in some juvenile attempt to make it look like a studio. Off to the side sits a rickety metal table with a camera and the props I saw in the photos—a lollipop, a doll, a silver dildo, crotch-less white panties, and a few other items.

Oh, I am going to have fun with you, Professor Kane Gregg.

From his condo, I drive back to the bar and I park in the lot. Across to the other side sits his green hatchback. Turning my engine off, I settle back to watch. If he doesn't make a move tonight, I have a few new ideas on how to handle him.

I begin to visualize all the positions I'm going to pose him in, and right as I'm imagining one that involves the lollipop, I get a call from Reggie.

Still, with my attention on the green hatchback, I answer, "Hey."

"I figured it out—the degraded DNA sample."

I sit up a little. "And?"

"The woman who died in the house forty years ago used to babysit your mom. The woman had a daughter a few years older named Marjoream. Your mom was hiding in the closet when the murder occurred. She would have been five and Marjoream eight. Apparently, Marjoream was asleep on the couch and she woke up to find her mother butchered. Though if you ask me, I don't know how Marjoream slept through that. She was probably drugged.

Either way, your mom, Lane, saw it all happen from her spot in the closet. Marjoream then got in the closet with your mom. They were too scared to do anything else. They hid in that closet the entire night. Your grandmother showed up the following morning to pick your mom up and found the murdered babysitter.

Your mom didn't give an accurate enough description, probably because the poor thing was traumatized. The investigators believed she was confused at what she saw and ruled it a suicide. Your grandparents, though, believed your mom and that there had been a murder that occurred. They were scared the killer would come after the girls next and so they changed their names and moved to another city.

Your grandparents ended up adopting Marjoream and the girls were raised as sisters. And, of course, your grandparents died when your mom was in her early twenties." Reggie stops talking. "Holy shit, right?"

"To the nth degree."

"There's one more thing." Reggie takes a breath. "Somewhere along the way, Marjoream dropped off the radar. Who knows, perhaps she had lingering fear the killer would one day find her and your mom."

Or the two of them became killers in their own right.

"She resurfaced in Richmond some time back under yet

another name. She was found stabbed to death outside of a trailer in the woods. In the trailer, a woman was held captive in a cage. There were also photos of other young people tortured to death. The local law linked Marjoream to several unsolved cases." Reggie pauses. "I'm sorry, Lane. This is horrible news."

"It is."

"I'm sure what Marjoream witnessed all those years ago shaped her into who she became. That's probably why your mom cut ties with her. Because after your grandparents died, there's little record of them every communicating again."

Or it was their elaborate plan to be monsters and exist off the radar.

"Well...I don't know what to say." I pause. "Thank you for digging around. That makes sense now as to why Mom's degraded DNA was found in that closet. Who knows, she may have had a nose bleed or bitten her fingernails raw."

"Do you think the FBI knew all of this? Victor? Oh, God, are you going to tell him?"

"Considering the FBI does thorough background checks, they had to know." I mean, who the hell knows? My mom was trained on how to hide facts and falsify information. "But, no, I truly believe Victor is in the dark. And, yes, I'm going to tell him, and Daisy, too."

"That doesn't sound like something you would do."

"Let's just say, we all had a bit of a 'come to Jesus' moment and I'm trying, really trying, to include them." Include them in everything but my mother's true identity as The Decapitator, and my true identity as her killer.

"That's good and a perfect lead into the other thing I want to tell you."

"The affair?" I guess.

"The what?"

"I found out that my mom and my real dad were having an ongoing affair and that Daisy is their daughter, too. That's the 'come to Jesus' moment we all had."

Reggie says, "I'm sorry, but that's not the picture I have of your mom. She walked on water in my eyes."

And I'm glad Reggie is now seeing a bit of the real and deceitful woman that my mother was. "You said there was something else?"

"Yeah. When I was digging around, I kept seeing the same IP addresses of two independent people doing the same digging. I traced them back to Victor and Daisy. Eventually, they are going to find out all of this about your mom and Marjoream. God, Lane, was it a mistake to look into all of this? We've dug up one too many skeletons. It's almost too much. I'm not sure I want to know more but somehow there is more."

"If there is I don't want to know it, so please stop digging. You found what I needed and I thank you. You're a great friend, Reggie."

"Are you disappointed in your mother?"

"Yes." I didn't even know her, really.

Reggie says, "She was a good woman and a mother, despite the affair. Always remember that. We all have secrets and that was her main one."

"Yeah, well, some secrets shouldn't be found out." If I could, I would destroy everything about her and close that door forever.

Reggie and I click off.

Across the bar parking lot, Professor Kane Gregg gets in his car alone. It looks like he's calling it a night. Alone.

Still, I follow him all the way back to his condo and I wait until he's inside and settled in for the night.

Good, because I really need to talk to Victor and Daisy.

44

I t's close to ten at night when I walk in our home. Both Victor and Daisy stay up until eleven, so I'm fairly sure I have an hour or so to talk with them.

But when I close the front door and slide my jacket off, I find Justin at the dining room table hunched over math homework.

It's way past his bedtime and I doubt Victor knows he's down here. I don't reprimand my brother, though, and instead, give him a hug.

He glances up at me through hazel eyes the exact color of Victor's. "What was that for?"

"Because I love you, and I will always love you, no matter what." I kiss the crown of his head, inhaling his freshly washed hair. "Where's Dad and Daisy?"

"Dad had a headache and went to bed about an hour ago. Daisy is taking a long bath and doesn't want to be disturbed." Justin rolls his eyes.

Smiling, I pull out a chair and sit down beside him. I note he's stepping his way through equations. Math is my thing, and the one subject I've always helped Justin with. I pick up a pencil and with a nod, he slides his paper over.

As I always do, I walk him through, line-by-line, and carefully, he listens. He's a follower, not a leader, which is why he fell prey to the bullies at school.

But I learned a long time ago Justine thrives when he feels in control, like right now as he independently does the next equation. These are the type of things that boost his confidence.

"Was thinking we could work on some moves this weekend?" He's been struggling to level up in Aikido. A few pointers are all he needs.

He stops with the equation and glances over at me. "Really?"

I've been so focused on Daisy, school, Mom's secrets, and so many other things that I've taken for granted my brother didn't really need me. He needs my attention just as much as everything else. I can't forget him.

I need to get more and stay more involved with him. "Really."

He grins. "Cool."

We continue working for the next thirty minutes or so until he begins yawning and I send him up to bed.

I'm glad I came by, but I still need that conversation with Victor and Daisy.

I leave a quick note for Victor:

Came by to talk to you and Daisy. When is good?

45

The next night I'm back at Wish You Were Beer Bar, this time inside. College students pack the place, most halfway toward full inebriation. A local blues band occupies the back wall, thumping their way through a deep and slow song. In one corner a few students play pool. In another, others play darts. In the center, a few dance. At the bar, the stools are packed with drinkers crowded in behind.

Standing room only.

I choose a spot near the dart boards, leaning back all casual like, tapping my foot to the slow beat, and staring straight across the place to where Professor Kane Gregg stands beside a girl perched on a stool.

She's laughing. He's laughing. Life is so funny when you're drinking and flirting.

Thanks to the sedative I stole from Patch and Paw's supply closet, I'm ready for this guy. He slips the girls a mickey, I'm slipping him one. He's going to experience every single thing that he does to them. Tonight is the night.

A beefy wrestler type guy slides up beside me. "Hey, haven't seen you here before."

I smile a little.

He glances at my empty hands. "I'll get you something. What's your poison?"

Tonight my poison is Professor Kane Gregg. Drugged. Stripped naked. Posed and exposed for the camera. But of course, that's not what this guy means. "Just water. Thank you."

"Cool." With that, he heads off.

Good, I need my space. Professor Kane Gregg leans over, "accidentally" brushing the side of the girl's breast. She shrugs it off. He chuckles at his "mistake". Such a gentleman.

I glance around the packed bar, seeing several other older adults that are probably faculty or staff, too. Shouldn't there be a rule against this? Fraternizing, sure, but there's no rule about which bar what person goes to.

I spy the beefy wrestler guy still in line to get my water. That's fine. I'm here until Professor Kane Gregg makes a move. A loud crash draws my attention toward the pool table where a girl just knocked over several beer bottles perched on a ledge. But it's the person hovering in the dark corner who I zero in on.

Sabrina.

Sipping from a can of Sprite, she's trying to look all casual, but her stiff shoulders give her away. She's busy studying the bar and I doubt she's noticed me yet, but my gut tells me she's here for the same reason as me.

This is the last place Erna remembers and Sabrina is trying to piece together the puzzle. I thought I had some time to wait things out, but my roommate just upped the clock.

160   S. E. GREEN

A pack of students move in front of me and using them for cover, I skirt out and around to exit through the door. Outside in the parking lot, I know exactly where Professor Kane Gregg parked his green hatchback and a new plan forms.

I stop a guy going into the bar. "Hi, do you know Professor Kane Gregg?"

"Yes."

"Will you tell him I saw someone key his car?"

"Sure."

The guy disappears inside and I walk straight through the dimly lit lot to wait by Professor Kane Gregg's car. Pulling my phone out, I give it a quick glance, but Victor still hasn't texted me about the note I left. That's fine, he's busy. If I don't hear from him tonight, I'll check in tomorrow.

Tucking my phone away, I slide a flask from my jacket pocket loaded with whiskey-laced sedative, or sedative-laced whiskey. Either way, it'll do the job.

Slipping up on the hood of his green hatchback, I kick back and take a pretend swig from the flask.

He marches toward me. "Excuse me!"

I glance over, all innocent, and with my practiced Russian accent, I respond. "Yez?"

"This is my car. What are you doing?"

"Oh!" I glide off the hood. "I thought et vaz my friend'z car."

With an annoyed sigh, he walks the perimeter, looking for the key marks, and apparently appeased that there's been a reported mistake, he circles back around to where I stand next to his hood.

I take another fake swig from the flask. "Iz okay?"

Cocking his head, he studies me and I keep right on smiling. Up close, he really is a good looking man.

"Where you from?" he asks.

"Rossia."

"You an exchange student?"

I nod, taking another fake drink. He eyes the flask, and I take that as my cue. I hold it out to him. "Iz cold out, no? Please, iz vheskiy."

He moves in closer, taking the flask, making sure his fingers brush mine. "Thanks." He takes a sip, and then another, and I take it back from him. I want him loopy, not passed out.

Recapping the flask, I slide it back into my coat pocket and I step further into him, forcing him back against the hood. His eyes widen a little with my aggressive stance.

I arch a brow. "Leve around here?"

Professor Kane Gregg is already digging his keys out of his jeans pocket as he says, "Yes."

Pressing a kiss to his neck, I pluck the keys from his fingers. "Let mi."

He chuckles and chuckles, and I smile and smile. A bit of a lightweight, this one.

Without me even helping him, he climbs into the passenger side and I slide into the driver's. I let his hands get all grabby as I turn the hatchback on and slowly pull from the lot. He doesn't think to give me directions but I prompt him anyway, even though I know my way.

By the time we arrive at his condo, he is good and buzzed and nearly passed out. I hope I didn't underestimate the sedative's effect.

Once I'm in the garage with the door closed and the engine off, I search his pockets and find the Rohypnol he would have used tonight if given the chance.

Opening the driver's door, I climb out and I circle

around to get him out, too. "Come on, Professor Gregg. Showtime."

With a half-baked grin, he smooshes his finger into my cheek. "You don't have an accent anymore."

I unzip his jacket and slide it down his arms. "So why don't you tell me about all the girls you bring here."

He turns a slow circle, letting me take the jacket off. "I like taking pictures of girls."

"Yes, you do." I grasp the hem of his long sleeve Henley. "Arms up."

He listens, and I tug his shirt off. "Can you do your jeans?"

"Yepper." He unbuttons and unzips, hopping around a bit as he works them down his legs.

I nod over to the mattress with the red satin sheet. "Is that where you do it?"

"Oh, yeah." He gets his jeans off and strips his boxers without me asking as he walks toward the mattress.

Naked he plops down, and I pick up the camera already waiting on the metal table.

"Show me what you have the girls do," I say.

Laughing, he rolls over, spreading his legs and giving me a rear view. I lift the camera and click. Not the best view, but whatever.

"What else?" I prompt.

And he proceeds to show me every disgusting thing he makes the girls do.

With the lollipop.

The crotch-less panties.

The dildo.

The baby doll.

And I take pictures of it all.

When he's done showing me everything, I help him get dressed and help him walk up the stairs into his condo. "Who are you?" he mumbles as I assist him into his unmade bed.

"I'm the person who is making you pay for what you did to all those innocent girls."

"Oh."

Oh, indeed.

With a yawn, he rolls over. "I shoot them because they're pretty. They should thank me because now they live on forever in photos so unique people share them."

I almost turn and leave, but his words stop me. I look down at him all drunk on the sedative and compliant. I really do need to punch him.

And so I do, hard, over and over again, wishing he were more alert to experience this. At least he'll feel it in the morning.

Disgusting human being.

I leave him just like he left all the girls, fully dressed and passed out, only to wake up in the morning unsure of how he got home.

I take the memory card from the camera, walk straight out his front door, and the two miles back to the bar where my Jeep still sits parked in the lot.

Now to upload the photos and make an anonymous call that his place should be searched.

. . .

By noon the next day, the pictures are everywhere and Sabrina finds me in the cafeteria eating a burrito.

She slides her finger across her phone and shows me one. "Can you believe this?"

"Huh, look at that." I dunk my burrito in guacamole and take a bite.

"That's Professor Kane Gregg."

"I see that."

"He's the last person Erna remembers talking to." Sabrina waves the phone in my face. "He took those pictures and someone got him back. They even searched his place and found evidence. He's been arrested."

"Sounds like he got what he deserved."

For a moment, Sabrina stands beside me, quietly watching me eat my burrito. I keep eating, glancing up every so often. Finally, I ask, "Anything else?"

She grins. "No." Then she shocks the hell out of me when she grabs my face and gives me a loud kiss.

I pull back. "What the hell, Sabrina?"

Still, with the grin, she plops down across from me. "Glad we're friends, that's all." She swipes a finger through my guacamole and tastes it. "Mm."

I roll my eyes and she laughs. Okay, I'll admit it, I'm glad we're friends, too.

As she gets up to go buy her own burrito, a text finally comes in from Victor: CAN YOU COME BY THE HOUSE TONIGHT?

YES, I type back.

Time to tell them what I found out from Reggie.

46

That night, I sit in our living room beside Daisy. Victor sent Justin upstairs to take a shower, and silently I watch Victor pacing. Something tells me he already knows everything I want to tell him.

As soon as the shower turns on, he stops pacing and looks first at my sister and then me.

"This stays between the three of us. Justin is too young to know. I'll tell him when the time is right." Victor takes a breath. "The degraded sample." He looks at me. "Do you remember when we discussed Marji, a childhood friend of your mother's?"

I look at Daisy. "We know they were sisters."

Victor pauses. "How do you know that?"

Shifting forward on the couch, I brace my elbows on my knees. I'm not entirely sure what he knows and how much of it matches up to Reggie's information, but I go ahead. "I had Reggie look into everything when I heard about the degraded sample. I only just found out and planned on telling you two everything. This is what I know..."

I step them through everything. Mom and Marji, childhood friends, Mom watching the murder of Marji's mother, and the two of them hiding in the closet because they were too scared to come out. Mom's parents taking Marji in and adopting her. The whole family changing their names and moving. Mom and Marji going separate ways when they got older. And Marji later being found stabbed outside the trailer where she tortured so many young people.

When I get done, I look over at Daisy to find her staring at a photo on the mantel of our family taken a few years ago on a hike we did in the Shenandoah Valley.

With a sigh, Victor sits down on the ottoman. "The FBI needs to hire Reggie."

That they do.

"And you didn't know any of this?" Daisy asks Victor.

"No." He shakes his head. "Your mom never told me any of this."

She looks at me. "And how long have you known?"

"I literally just found out."

My sister pushes off the couch. She crosses over to the coat rack, slips on her winter jacket and gloves, and walks right out the front door.

I expected tears, a flare of temper, possible shouting, or more questions, but none of that occurs. I get up to go after her, and Victor waves me down.

"Let me," he says, and I nod.

It's probably for the best. My sister and I only just made up and this just makes things more fragile.

I find my way into the kitchen and as I make a cup of coffee, I survey Victor's closed office door.

The last time I checked, there was nothing in there but normal stuff. It doesn't hurt to check again.

I try the handle and find it locked. He never locks the office door. There's something in there he doesn't want us to see. My gut tells me it's about Mom. I have to break in. It's the only way to stay one step ahead.

A quick glance out the blinds of our living room shows Victor and Daisy down the block, walking away from our house. Upstairs, Justin shuts his bedroom door. I have to work quickly.

I don't have my lock picks on me but from the kitchen, I find a paper clip and a butter knife.

Just like Victor taught me how to use lock picks, he also taught me how to use household items to do various things: picking locks, using a newspaper as a weapon, expanding soap in a microwave, using steel wool for a light show...

It takes me seconds longer than usual, but when the handle releases, I breathe out. Yes.

The kitchen light filters in behind me and illuminates the small room. I take one step inside, and I freeze.

My gaze bounces off the walls, the desk, the floor, the file cabinets. Everything covered with notes, drawings, pictures, maps, and lists of various killers that Mom helped catch over the years.

It's like looking inside of her dark and disturbed mind.

Where did all of this come from, and why is Victor revisiting it?

Is there a new killer I'm not aware of? Is this FBI business?

No, I don't think so. Victor rarely brings his work home.

The word SUICIDE? draws my attention over to the wall to read notes in Victor's writing:

DNA profile from hair strand (a link between all three suicides) points toward Caucasian of northern European descent. Same killer Suzie and Marji witnessed? If so, approximate age would be 60 to 70 years old. Why is the killer back and where has he been?

168

S. E. GREENS. E. GREEN

He's been all over, killing in his evil cycle of suicides.
I shift away from those notes to look at the next set.

THE DECAPITATOR.

MY BREATH HITCHES.

"Shit." Victor isn't researching the killers Mom caught,
he's researching *her*.

47

As I drive back to the dorms, I don't think about what I just saw in Victor's office. Short of torching the place, there's not a whole lot I can do. And frankly, if he finds out Mom was a serial killer, it'll be a relief. I'll have someone else to share that burden with.

No, I don't think about that. For some reason, I do think about the man I accidentally killed several months back. He was the brother to my friend, Adam, and the son of the D. A.

I made a mistake in killing him. Mistakes happen. Granted, Adam's brother wasn't so innocent. He seduced many of his high school students and filmed them having sex. Granted the girls were willingly participating, but still.

Then why I am thinking about it right now?

Perhaps because Professor Kane Gregg got off on exploiting girls, too. Or perhaps because of the female social worker that Tommy and the BDAP recently took care of. Or, hell, maybe even because of the pedophile I served up justice to several months back.

They're all linked with exploitation and manipulation of others.

But Adam's brother wasn't a killer. He didn't deserve to die. He deserved justice more like what I did with Professor Kane Gregg.

Yet I accidentally killed Adam's brother and now I'm... uneasy. I want to take comfort that justice was served up, but I can't. It was the wrong type of justice.

Bart Novak is the right kind of justice and who I should be focused on. The Suicide Killer of single moms, dating back forty years. The first woman dies by cutting herself, the second an overdose, and the third a hanging. That's the pattern—done every November to mourn his mother's passing. Never linked because they are suicides. Yet this time he made sure to leave a strand of hair visible on each body. He wants the suicides connected.

Is he done?

Enough with this. It's time to finally take care of Bart Novak. There's no question of his guilt, and I need certainty right now. It'll get me back on track. It'll put an end to the last cycle that is my mother.

48

The next day I arrive at Aveda Retirement Home to find Bart outside stringing up holiday lights. He offers me a bright smile. "Hi, Maggie. Didn't think you were on the schedule today."

So, he's looking at my schedule. Interesting.

Hiking my book bag over my shoulder, I smile right back. "I'm not, but I wanted to see how you're doing after the squirrel."

"Oh, aren't you sweet." He loops a light string around a lamp post. "No need to dwell. I've put it out of my mind already."

He glimpses beyond me to where a maintenance man clips a bush. "No, no, no." Bart slides past me, grabbing the clippers from the man's hand. "Like this at the stem. You're taking too much off."

"Got it," the man says.

"Well, if you've got it, then why do I have to keep showing you?" Bart slaps the clippers back into the man's gloved hand and nods him to continue.

You'd think Bart owns the place with the way he orders people around.

Holleen, the desk clerk, steps out the front door, catches sight of us, and jogs over. She hands Bart car keys and a credit card. "Your car is gassed and ready."

He pockets the keys and the card. "Where's my receipt?"

She cringes. "Oops, forgot that. You can just look on your credit card statement, though." She grins, all helpful.

His jaw muscles flex. "Next time get a receipt."

Her grin slides away.

Bart turns back to his string of lights, and quietly, Holleen makes her way back inside.

I ask, "Going somewhere?"

"Yes, just to the other side of town. I have a few things to take care of."

Other side of town. Few things to take care of. Nice vague answers. Answers I tend to give when asked. Which makes me think...is this Suicide Killer type stuff? Is this part of the ritual? Does he revisit the suicide scenes?

Whatever it is, I need to come up with a reason to go with him, because this might be the opportunity I've been waiting for. The window needed to take care of him, for good. But what does one use for a last minute kill? I'll have to improvise. I do have a few supplies in my book bag...

The maintenance man's phone rings. As he answers it, he walks around the side of the building for privacy, leaving me and Bart alone.

Perfect.

Stepping back, Bart surveys his work with the light string and apparently pleased, he pulls the keys back out of his flannel jacket and turns toward the parking lot.

A quick look in the maintenance man's direction shows

him out of sight. Yes, perfect. No one will see me leave with Bart.

I step up beside him. "Mind if I tag along?"

He keeps walking. "I'm sorry, not this time."

"Please?"

Bart stops walking and turns to look at me.

"I like being with you. You remind me of my grandfather. He was a lot like you. He always had a purpose. Focus. Certainty. A generosity of spirit. Just like you."

Pushing his thick glasses up his nose, he sighs, a bit annoyed, but moving closer to relenting. "Don't you have any friends?"

"No."

"Alright." He nods to his car. "Come on."

I let him see all the relief in my face. "Thank you."

As I climb in, I look toward Aveda Home, double checking that no one saw us leave together. And if by chance someone did, that's okay. They know me as Maggie Cain, not Lane Cameron.

Bart Novak drives off, weaving his way through Alexandria, and eventually getting onto 495. I'm wrong. He's not revisiting the suicide scenes. He would have stayed in Alexandria for that.

He heads north. One exit goes by, and another, then another. The further we go away, the more a cloud lifts in anticipation of how this trip will end. I don't know all the ins and outs yet, but spontaneity can be good.

Interesting. Intriguing.

"So where we headed?" I ask.

"North."

With a chuckle, I point to the interstate sign. "495 north. That's evident."

He doesn't respond.

"I heard you haven't lived at Aveda for long. Move around a lot?"

"Here and there."

"Well, Aveda is a retirement home and so I guess you're here to stay. What are you retiring from?" I mean, other than killing. "Aren't you a writer?"

As a response, he grunts.

"So how do you like living at Aveda?" I ask.

"I don't know."

"What do you mean you don't know?"

He slides me an annoyed look. "I'm not in the mood for questions."

"Sorry," I mumble, all pathetic.

"Do I really remind you of your grandfather?"

"Yes, you do. He died a few years back."

"So no mother and no grandfather," he says.

"I guess that's why I feel such a connection to you."

"Because I remind you of your grandfather."

"Well, and..."

His brows lift. "And?"

I sigh. "I guess I'm not brave enough to say."

"How am I supposed to communicate with you if you don't talk to me? You asked to come with me. Generosity of spirit. Purpose. Focus. Certainty. Those are all the things you said just moments ago."

"Okay, fine. I feel a connection because both of our mothers are dead. Except..." I pause for dramatic effect, hoping I'm not taking this conversation too far, but also very curious of his response.

Bart veers north again. "Except?"

I don't respond.

He lets out an agitated sigh. "How about I exit and drop you off to fend for yourself? Because clearly, you don't want—"

"I lied to you. My mom didn't die of natural causes. She...she committed suicide."

Silence.

He looks at me. He looks at the road. His knuckles tighten around the wheel. "What happened?"

"I found her. She'd swallowed a stomach full of pills."

"It's not your fault."

"Still, it's left me with this feeling." I press a hand to my stomach. "I'm gutted from it."

He veers, circling back around the 495 loop. "It's a hard thing to bear. And now your conscience eats away at you with the 'what if's' and the 'why nots'."

"Yes." Is he going to tell me his mother committed suicide too?

"What you just did, telling me, is huge. It's good for the soul to talk about things."

Is it? Because I prefer not to talk. Maybe that means I have no soul.

"And you volunteering like you do at Aveda? That helps you score points with God."

I'll score more points if I rid the world of you, Mr. Novak. But I can't do anything if we don't get out of this car. I look around the interstate. Yep, we're circling back. Mentally, I catalog the items in my book bag: pepper spray, zip ties, taser, pocket knife, small screwdriver, lock picks, duct tape.

Not exactly what a girl might carry, but also not items to raise too much suspicion should the items be found. It's not how I ultimately want to do Mr. Novak, but again, improvising here. I don't want to miss a valuable opportunity.

He turns on his blinker, exiting right back into Alexandria. "I have a little surprise for you."

"I don't really like surprises."

"Yes, but this one will make you feel better."

My feet shift, tucking the book bag in closer. My items are tucked in the front pocket. Easy access.

"In fact—" He takes a deep breath in and blows it back out—"I'm lighter just thinking about it." He bounces his shoulders, all happy now. "Almost there."

First, he's jumping down everyone's throats and now he's happy. Or emotionally crumbling. It goes either way.

He turns another blinker on and excited murmurs pulse through my veins. We're almost to our destination.

Bart slows and parallel parks along the curb. He cuts the engine, reaches under his seat for a leather zipper pouch similar to a shaving kit, and climbs out. Grabbing my backpack, I follow. If he thinks it's odd I'm carrying a book bag, he doesn't say. Just like I don't mention the leather zipper pouch.

He comes to a stop in the dry front yard and stares at the small brick home where the first suicide/murder occurred. "I grew up here," he says.

He's done a lot more here than just grow up.

"Actually, I own it."

Well, that's something Reggie missed in her cyber digging.

"My tenant recently died," he says. "Very sad. She was a single mom. Committed suicide." Bart steps across the yard and up the few steps to the front door. "I've been wanting to come here since it happened but I haven't had a chance." Using his key, he unlocks the door and steps inside.

I follow.

The smell of a stuffy and closed up home sifts through my senses with an underlying twang of cleaner. Winter light filters in from the partially closed blinds and provides the only light.

A hallway leads to what I assume must be the bedrooms, but he walks left into a small living room where the woman's body was found. Whoever cleaned the place did a great job. Other than a freshly scrubbed wood floor, no evidence of the kill exists.

Bart points to an archway that leads into a small kitchen. "Mom used to stand with her shoulder propped in that archway and watch me play here on a throw rug that used to cover this floor."

"Sounds like a good memory," I say, turning a slow circle, looking for the closet where my mother hid.

"This is where I found her." He points directly down from where he stands. "The first time."

Right next to the front door sits a closet where Mom hid. It's a direct shot into the living room. She saw everything that happened as it was occurring. Then Marji woke up and found her mother. She joined Mom in that closet.

"Found who?" I ask, though of course I already know.

He points as he talks. "I came in the back door, crossed through the kitchen, walked under that archway, and found my mother laying right here. She had slit both of her wrists and was bleeding out. Right here where I used to play. I startled her. She didn't think I was coming home so soon. She begged me to let her go and I didn't listen. I saved her life. There was so much blood. She blamed me. Because of me, she was still here."

Something vulnerable flashes in his eyes. "She became a ghost after that, and I became obsessed with following her. I knew she would try again. And she did. Three days later she drove to a park a few miles from here and she swallowed a bunch of pills. Just like your mom did. But like the first time, I saved her again."

Bart pulls in a breath, flinching like it's uncomfortable to breathe. "She hated me even more for that time and became violent with me, screaming, hitting me, calling me names. I didn't recognize her. I knew she needed help. I was only fourteen and didn't know what to do."

"What about your father?" I quietly ask.

"Never knew him. It was just me and Mother. The pills —that was the second time. Then two nights later she snuck out of the house and as usual, I followed. But I was on my bike and she in her car. It was too late. I found her hanging from a tree down by the Potomac."

He lifts an intense, yet relieved face. "I've never told anyone the whole story until now. I wanted you to know that you're not alone with your grief. I see a lot of me in you."

This is not good.

He steps forward. "You and I, we share a common tragedy. Do you see? It allows us to speak the truth." Through his nose, he inhales, and after he blows it out, relief curls his lips. "Confession really is good. It unburdens the soul. What a revelation. Thanks to you."

Um...

Bart keeps looking at me, just a foot or so between us like he's waiting on me to say something. Though I have no clue what.

His relief falters. "You need to shed your remorse. We both do."

"And...and how do we do that?"

"There's only one way." He lifts the leather zipper pouch and every nerve in my body goes on full alert. What the hell is he doing? "It's time to finally complete the circle. I've been waiting for a sign. You're the sign."

He unzips the pouch and folds it open. Inside lays a scalpel, a bottle of pills, a thin rope already tied into a noose, and a lock of his mother's hair.

My entire body freezes. "What are you doing?"

Bart slides the scalpel free. "This is how I die. It's meant to be. Full circle." He nods to the pills. "And those are for you to complete your own circle."

He's making a suicide pact with me. No more remorse. Confession. Grief. He's saying goodbye. This is it. This is why he left those strands of hair. He knew he would be killing himself and wanted everything connected. This man is going to die and then the cops will figure the whole thing out.

I could agree to this, fake taking the pills all while watching him slice his neck. He'll bleed out. He'll be dead. The world will be free of this madman.

It's not how I envisioned this going down, but it's there.

Yet somehow I find myself putting my book bag down and stepping closer toward him. Carefully, I take the scalpel from his hand and zip the pouch back up. "Not like this. The solution to your remorse is not suicide. There is no circle to complete. This is not how you unburden yourself."

There is no circle to complete. I should listen to my own words.

His deep-set green eyes fill with grateful tears. "I thought I was meant to guide you, but I just realized that you're meant to guide me. Our paths have crossed for a reason. Just like I saved my mother, you've saved me." Taking my hand is his damp one, he squeezes it hard. "Thank you."

What am I doing? Why am I saving this man?

He chuckles. "I'm embarrassed. In fact, I'd appreciate it if you don't tell anyone back at Aveda about this. Our secret?"

More like my mistake because I'm already regretting it. "Sure, Bart."

He smiles, now at peace.

I frown, anything but.

Together we walk from the house, and as we cross the front yard back to his car, the hair on my neck shifts to stand. I search the old neighborhood.

There a few blocks down sits Mom's Lexus that Daisy now drives. I didn't see it when we first arrived. She must have pulled up while we were inside.

Some subscribe to the saying "Everything happens for a reason". I've never once. I'm more of a "You make shit happen" type of thinker.

But stopping Bart from ending his life? That happened for a reason.

And Daisy is that reason.

49

Bart and I drive back to Aveda, him chatting the whole way and me silent—opposite of how we were when we started this journey.

He came back here to Alexandria to complete the fifty-year cycle. He left his mother's hair in memoriam because he had no intention of living any longer. He didn't care if the cops figured things out. He knew he was leaving this world.

He's still leaving this world, but it'll be by my hand.

Not by his. Mine.

Bart and I arrive at Aveda, and he's still chatting away. "How about a game of Tri-Onimoes? You ever played? It's very fun!"

With Daisy at the forefront of my mind, I make an excuse. "I'm sure it is, but—" I rub my belly— "I'm not feeling very well."

His face falls. "Oh. Okay..."

"Next time," I say.

He all but slinks into Aveda, all bummed out. Whatever.

I grab the first bus I can back to where I parked my Jeep. Daisy.

Daisy. Daisy. Daisy.

I don't even want to think of how that would have gone down if I walked from that house to leave Bart Novak dead and bled out in the living room. As it stands now, my brain scrambles for an explanation to tell her.

I call her. I text her. She doesn't answer.

I drive by all the places she might be: home, friends, high school campus, Starbucks… and on a last thought, I go to a park north of McLean where our parents used to take us to play.

As I pull in to the parking lot, I catch sight of her sitting alone in the middle of a soccer field. I park beside her car, glad to find the place empty and private.

Pulling out my binoculars, I zero in on her and the cardboard box sitting beside her. She reaches inside, selects a photo, flicks a lighter, and burns it. Next, she pulls out a pink playdough project that she and Mom made when Daisy was a little kid. She places it in the dried grass, picks up a hammer that I just now notice lays beside her, and she bangs it to pieces.

For several minutes she keeps this up—burning photos, shredding papers, banging objects. I don't have to be closer to know this is about Mom. I could go to Daisy. Stop her. But I don't.

I did the exact same thing.

So I sit right here in my Jeep, giving her space and at the same time, making sure she's alright.

Roughly thirty minutes later, she leaves the remnants right where they are and holding the hammer, she pushes to her feet. She turns toward the parking lot, finally catches sight of me, and pauses.

Opening my door, I get out.

As she walks toward me I try to read her face, but it is void of all emotion.

Still holding the hammer, she comes to a stop right in front of me, and for the first time in my life, I experience a flare of fear with Daisy.

Her knuckles tighten around the handle. "Did you know Mom snapped one of my cheerleading trophies in half?"

I frown. "What?"

"She and I were having an argument and she lost it. She picked up that trophy, snapped it in half, and threw it at me." My sister points to a tiny scar on her cheek.

Mom told us that Daisy tripped and banged herself on the corner of the dresser. "Daisy..." I reach for her. "I had no idea."

She steps from my reach. "It wasn't the first time." My sister barks a laugh. "Remember when I 'fell' horseback riding and got a black eye?"

"Yes," I whisper.

"That time she hit me with her briefcase."

Oh my God.

Turning, Daisy paces over to Mom's car and with a yell, she swings the hammer and crashes it into the hood. "Then there was the time she broke my pinky finger."

No.

With another yell, the hammer makes contact with the left headlight.

"But not you. Oh, no. You were the favorite." The hammer crashes into the other headlight.

My heart sinks. "I didn't know."

Both hands grip the handle and Daisy raises the hammer above her head, this time bringing it down into the windshield. "Of course you didn't know. No one knew. And plus, who would believe me? Mom was the fucking FBI

Director and hero of the universe, and I was just the difficult daughter."

"I would have believed you. Dad would have believed you."

Gritting her jaw, she paces to the back of the car and she whacks the rear lights. She turns the hammer, sharp end out, and she pummels the tire. Over and over and over again.

My soul aches for her and I want to go to her, to hug her. But I don't. She won't accept it right now.

She points the hammer at me. "And don't you dare tell Dad. His heart is already broken enough over Mom."

"I won't," I assure her. "If he finds out, it'll be by you, not me."

Rounding the car, she starts in on another tire. "I argued with her. I fought with her. I brought it on. But you never did. I thought you were her favorite because you were Seth's daughter. But I'm Seth's too!"

"She had no right to hurt you, Daisy."

Breathing heavy, she looks at me. "You have no idea what she was really like. None of you do. You don't know what she was capable of."

Oh, but I do.

With another yell, Daisy throws the hammer and it sails through the air to skid across the parking lot. "Everyone thought we were such a perfect family. And just look at us? You know what, I'm glad she's dead."

I am, too.

Daisy yanks the keys from her coat pocket and tosses them onto the hood. She rounds the Jeep and climbs in. I don't ask her what she's doing. I already know. She doesn't want anything of Mom's, including her car.

Opening my driver's door, I climb back in. "We'll tell Dad it was stolen."

"Fine." Daisy clips on her seatbelt.

I crank the engine and slowly drive from the lot. The perfect family. The happy family. The normal family. How can you really know? How can you know if the mom is really loving or just wearing a mask? How can you tell if the sister is really "difficult" or acting out because she's frightened? How can you really tell anything?

It's more like everyone is a bomb waiting to go off. Nothing is perfect. Is it ever?

"What were you doing at that house?" My sister asks.

"I've been volunteering at a local old folks' home. I've grown close to one of the residents and he agreed to see that house with me."

"I should have gone in with you the day you took me there," Daisy says.

"It's okay. I understood."

"What was it like?"

"Sad. I saw the closet where Mom was hiding when they saw Marji's mother murdered."

"Do you think that shaped them into who they became?"

"One of many things, I'm sure."

After Mom's death, Daisy went through this period where she idolized her. So much so it annoyed me. Looking back on that, I think my sister was doing what she thought was expected. Perhaps she shoved all the bad stuff down in order to be a "good" daughter and sister. I get that.

Sensing she'll accept my touch now, I reach over and squeeze her knee. "I love you, Daisy. We're going to get through this."

But she doesn't answer and instead stares out the window as we drive home.

50

After I drop my sister off, I drive back to the dorms. From under my seat, I take out the file of information on the Suicide Killer. A quick glance around the parking lot shows I'm alone. The last thing I need is a student walking by and peering in to see my work.

I look through photos of the victims and it's like a damn family portrait.

All young single mothers and representing the cycle of Bart's mother.

How, though, does he come across all these women? How does he get close enough to pull this off?

I scroll through Mom's notes again. *Lacks insight into how he engages with others. Does not understand concept of boundary. Avoids responsibility for his conduct. Preys on emotional sensitivity. A master at creating scenarios. Pretends to be a good person.*

It describes Bart, for sure. But are these notes based on her memory of seeing him or on her general thoughts? I don't know. Everything is written as if formally done. Not from a personal perspective.

The fact is, I know who the killer is. That is an absolute certainty. The question is how does he interact with all these women? How do they trust him enough to let him near?

The kid has to be the key.

It takes time to get to know your victim and their patterns. Now that I've given him a new lease on life, I'd say he's thinking of next November and a new round of kills. But now he lives here in Alexandria in a retirement home. He's no longer mobile. Which means next year's victims will likely be within driving distance of Aveda.

Virginia, Maryland, D.C... A lot of possibilities.

Given the fact he left his mother's hair behind, though, in what was supposed to be his final act, things may change now. His ritual may become different. Hell, he may start cycling the kills as soon as a month from now.

I flip one last time through the folder, wishing Mom would have kept more personal notes, especially on what she witnessed as a child. As much as I want him dead, I'm also curious about the process.

Closing my eyes, I rest my head on the seatback. Suicide. Murder. When I was with him in that house, he offered the pills to me. He wanted me to take my own life. Going with that, what if he doesn't actually do the killing? What if he gets the single mother to kill her own self?

Killing, but not really, because he's not actually doing the deed. He's not making it look like suicide because it truly is. The perfect serial killer—somehow he gets the mother to take her own life.

How, though? What are the words that he says?

If he threatens to kill the kid, that can't be enough. I mean, who's to say he won't kill the kid anyway after the mom commits suicide? If I were a mom, I would want proof my kid was going to live.

Proof.

What type of proof would Bart give? What type of proof would I accept if I was about to kill myself to save my kid?

My phone buzzes with a text from Tommy: DID YOU FORGET THAT YOU HAVE A BOYFRIEND? ;)

Despite the fact I currently have a folder of the Suicide Killer opened on my lap, I still smile. SORRY, LIFE HAS BEEN BUSY.

I'D LIKE TO THINK THAT A BENEFIT OF DATING IS THAT I'M NOT ALONE EVERY NIGHT. WHAT ARE YOU DOING RIGHT NOW? I BOUGHT JELL-O...

Jell-O. Code for fooling around. I GUESS I'M IN THE MOOD FOR DESSERT. BE THERE IN AN HOUR.

DOOR WILL BE UNLOCKED. COME ON IN.

I first started dating Tommy with an idea of role-playing. I was a daughter, a sister, a student, a friend, and I added girlfriend to that list. But now it's so much more.

Putting my notes away, I head into the dorm. I'll likely spend the night with Tommy and so I'll pack a bag and be on my way.

But when I walk into our room, Zach and Sabrina are spread across her bed, sharing earbuds and listening to music while working on what looks like an art project.

Well, this is interesting.

Sabrina plucks her earbud out. "Hey!"

"Hey back." I look between them. "I didn't realize you two were friends."

Zach takes his earbud out, too. "We've been hanging for a few days now." He bumps his shoulder against Sabrina. "You've got a fun roommate."

With a slight blush to her cheeks, Sabrina waves him off. I look between them again—Zach with his boy-next-door scruffy cuteness and Sabrina with her big adorable dimples—and, yeah, I can see this. They're way beyond cute.

Sabrina sends me a playful cringe and I nod. All good. I'm totally fine with them hanging and possibly dating if they want. "I'm just going to grab a few things."

"You don't have to leave!" Sabrina climbs off the bed. She picks up what looks like a fighter pilot mask and waves it at me. "I've been wearing this for days now and you haven't noticed." Her brows lift. "The snoring?"

"Oh, yeah, I have noticed. Just didn't realize you were wearing that."

"Better?"

"Yes, much better. Thank you for doing that."

"So then don't leave. Stay."

"It's not that, Tommy asked me over."

"Oh!" She grins. "Well, then."

Zach's not even paying us attention as he picks up a photo and slides it into a multi-sectioned frame. He holds it up to show Sabrina. "What do you think?"

She sighs. "That's perfect. I love that you put him right in the middle." She looks at me. "Zach's helping me organize photos for my mom's Christmas present." She points to the photo of the handsome dark-haired man in the middle. "That's my Uncle Gene, my mom's younger brother. He died a few years back."

"How'd he die?"

"Um...murdered actually."

"Any idea who did it?"

Zach glances up. "Jesus, Lane. Can't you even say you're sorry?"

God, he's right. "I'm sorry."

Sabrina shakes her head. "It's okay," she whispers.

I'm a horrible friend. I should have never asked her that.

Changing the subject would probably be a good thing. "Hey, how's it going with your family? Any luck on the extracurricular activities?"

My roommate puts her snore mask back down. "Yes." Her smile is back, and I'm so glad to see it. "Thanks for that advice."

"Sure thing."

She takes her seat beside Zach and they continue working. As I pack my overnight bag, I watch them interact, and just hearing their bright voices and soft laughter lightens my soul.

As I'm putting my toothbrush on top of my bag I find myself doing something very out of character as I say, "Hey, Sabrina, do you like zip lining? Maybe we could do that sometime."

She looks up from the art project and her face brightens. "That sounds great!"

"Cool." I grab my bag and walk from the room, smiling.

It's a real smile, not a fake one.

51

The following afternoon I stroll into Aveda and straight up to the front desk where Holleen, the clerk, sits. "Good afternoon." I sign in.

"Oh, hey, Maggie. I hear you helped Mr. Novak cut down the Christmas trees."

"That I did." I lay the pen aside. "He's really something, isn't he? He's got a big heart. Always giving back."

"Yes, that he does." Holleen grins. "He keeps busy, that's for sure."

I lean up against the desk. "Oh, yeah? Other than around here, what else does he do?"

"Oh goodness, a little bit of everything. There's not a day he's idle. In fact, he just recently signed up to volunteer with one of those Mommy and Me clubs." She laughs. "Can you imagine?"

A day not idle. Volunteer. Mommy and Me.

Her words click things into place. He picks organizations to worm himself into, like Mommy and Me. Groups that will put him around women with children. The cycle starts every year right after his November kills. He gets to know his next victims, carefully selecting them, earning their trust. And then the following year he carries out his kills.

Son of a bitch. That's how he cements himself into the victim's life. "Lot on his plate, that man. When does he do that?"

"Oh, in a few hours he'll leave."

I push off the desk. "So where is Mr. Novak? Love to say hi."

The phone rings, and holding her finger up to me, Holleen answers it.

"I'm right here." Bart walks across the lobby, dressed in his thick flannel as if ready to go outside. "I was just about to begin decorating those trees."

"Your tradition," I remind him.

"So is others helping, but apparently everyone around here is too busy."

"Well, I'm glad to."

"I see someone recognizes the importance of tradition." His glares at Holleen, still on the phone.

He has quite the thumb on the staff around this place. I step into his line of sight. "So where are they?"

"Just outside. I spent time yesterday setting them up."

"Great." I motion him on. "Lead the way."

I follow him across the lobby toward the automatic door that leads out to the back patio.

"Oh, Mr. Novak!" Holleen hangs up the phone as she points to a poinsettia sitting near her computer. "Thank you for the lovely decoration."

To her, he grunts. To me, he mumbles, "I'm glad someone thinks to show gratitude for the things I do around here."

The sensor opens the sliding glass door, and he steps out to the patio. I glance back at Holleen. From her wary expression, she heard what he said. But this isn't the first time he's spoken to her in this tone. Why does she allow it?

"Perhaps when we're done decorating, you can help me with a puzzle I've been puzzling over." He laughs. "Get it?"

"Yeah. Or play cards. I saw canasta on the schedule for later." I have no clue how to play canasta, but whatever.

"No, I only do puzzles in the winter. I've always only done puzzles in the winter. It's tradition. Just like the three trees. If everyone did whatever they wanted, there would be no sense of order. It's important to have order. It's important not to ignore tradition."

Like killing every November on the anniversary of your mother's suicide?

He stops walking and I nearly bump into his back. He turns to me as if an idea just came. "What are you thankful for, Maggie?"

Um, okay. "I'm...thankful for health and life."

Bart smiles a little. "What else?"

"For this volunteer job that has introduced me to so many wonderful people."

His smile falters. "What else?"

Jesus Christ, what is going on? "For animals. I love animals."

His smile drops away. "That's it?"

"Yes...?"

His eyes narrow.

"And you, of course. I'm most thankful for my new-found friendship with you."

A smile creeps back into his face. "And I you."

What the hell?

He turns away, stepping around outdoor furniture. "Hey!" Bart screams, and I jerk to attention.

He races across the patio in the direction of the three

trees and it takes me a second to register what is going on. There's a medium sized white dog with his leg lifted as he piddles on the lower branches of one of the trees.

"You stupid dog!" Bart yells, rearing back and sinking the toe of his old man tennis shoe into the dog's ribs.

Oh, he goddamn did *not* do that.

With a yelp and a whine, the dog rolls across the brick flooring and his little back hits a wall. I fly across the patio right as Bart gives chase, kicking the dog again.

"You stupid bastard!" he screams.

The dog scrambles to get away. Bart grabs a handful of his white fur, ready to propel it through the air, and in that exact second, I reach them.

Snatching a broom from the corner of the patio, I wrap it around from behind and I yank Bart back. His body catches air and the dog sprints off.

I hold the broom firm across his chest, wishing it was his neck. Bart kicks, gaining balance, and I let him go. He whirls on me and I flip the broom, handle side out, and ram it into his ribs. Just like he did with the dog. With a gasp, he stumbles back, losing his footing, and he falls down right next to his trees.

I twirl the broom, gaining a new grip, and ram him again in the ribs. "How does that feel, *bastard*?"

Bart yelps, scrambling away, whimpering. His skin colors up with fear. "No, please, stop."

I look into his pleading eyes and it only serves to cement my resolve. I take a step, stalking now, and something flutters in my chest. One side of my lips kicks up. I have been waiting for this. "I know who you really are. I should have killed you when I had the chance."

From across the patio comes a voice. "Stop! What are you doing?" Footsteps race toward me.

I freeze. What *am* I doing?

Still staring into Bart's fear-filled eyes, I lower the broom.

Holleen pushes past me, coming down next to Bart. "Oh my God! Daddy, are you okay?"

Daddy?

"I told you not to call me that." With a grunt, he sits up, looking beyond her to where I still stand. Or rather lurk. "You need to go."

My teeth grind together and I lift the broom, holding it like a baseball bat, and I swing hard at his stupid trees. One of them snaps in half and it provides a modicum of satisfaction. I carry the broom straight across the patio, back inside, across the lobby, and out the automatic front door.

It isn't until I'm standing at the bus stop that I note I still have the broom. I close my eyes, breathing out. He's destroyed so many families and he's terrorized everyone into being his friend and "respecting" him. Even his daughter, which...what the hell?

She's his human shield. For that matter, everyone who knows him personally plays that role. No one is brave enough to challenge him.

I showed him who I am. I told him I knew who he was.

He'll see me coming now. I had a chance to get rid of him early on, and now I'm no longer at the advantage.

52

A few hours later, I sit in my Jeep at the far end of Aveda's parking lot, staring at his beige four-door.

I didn't remember what happened to me as a child until I was forced to. Daisy seems the opposite. She remembers but pretends that she doesn't.

My darkness was born that day when I was just a toddler and I witnessed my birth parents slaughter one of their victims. Daisy's darkness is slowly evolving.

Bart Novak's darkness was born surrounding his mother's suicide attempts.

He's a man of ritual and tradition. He wakes up every morning. Eats breakfast. Does his freelance writing job. Eats lunch. Does his Tai Chi. Volunteers. Eats dinner. Goes to bed surrounded by his hair pillow and his cane of trophies as he contemplates his disturbing life. If he gets crazy, he may mix up the volunteering with the writing or Tai Chi.

Daddy, are you okay?

I told you not to call me that.

But somewhere along the way, he had a daughter that

was so far off my radar that I'm not sure anyone else even knows.

A man of ritual, which means any minute now, and despite the fact I hurt his ribs, he'll be leaving for his Mommy and Me venture.

The side door opens and out steps Bart, right on time. Dressed in his usual thick flannel, he pulls a beanie down over his balding head, slides his hands into black leather gloves and takes a second to look around the large parking lot.

A sea of vehicles packs the lot. He can't see me, but still, I slide down in my Jeep.

Inside his car, he sits for a minute or so, letting things warm up, before pulling from the lot.

At a safe distance, I follow as he winds his way through Alexandria, getting onto 495, and eventually exiting in Tysons. He pulls through traffic, cutting into the mall, and parks in the multi-level garage in the only available spot.

Crap.

I circle around, heading up one level, park near the steps, and I'm out of my Jeep and racing down before he's even crossed the walkway to go inside the mall.

In my cargo pants, I'm carrying the usual supplies plus one more—a thin noose. But there's no way I'm using them in a public mall.

As I follow him through the crowd, I pull my red curls into a quick ponytail. He cuts off down an escalator and I wait several seconds before descending, too. People pack the place, but I won't lose him.

From several steps up the escalator, I watch him watch others. I recognize the keen perception on his face. The aggressive eagerness. The desire for dark satiation.

Between stopping him from committing suicide and the confrontation over the dog, I've set him in motion.

I'm not the only one on a stalk.

He exits the escalator, circles around, and enters the food court. My focus shifts right and left, looking for a Mommy and Me gathering. Instead, he approaches a popcorn cart where Holleen, his *daughter,* currently stands.

They share a bag of popcorn that she already bought. I study them closely, gauging their relationship. I sense space between them, a careful distance that Bart works at keeping and probably always has. An eagerness, too, on her side. She's excited to be part of his life. Perhaps this is the first time he's allowed it.

It might be why he moved back to Alexandria. The 50th anniversary of his mother's death. Holleen was here. He planned on killing himself. He was making his own twisted amends. Yes, lots of reasons to come back.

I don't know Holleen's age, but I'd place her as the same as my mom—mid to late forties. Which means Bart had her before he began his cycle of kills.

Where, and who is her mom?

Together they walk across the food court to where a group of women and children have gathered. The Mommy and Me group.

Holleen Ickert, Aveda Home Desk Clerk, how exactly are you involved in your father's dual life? Do you know what is going on? Does he use you for cover? Are you clueless or in the know?

They walk up to the group and everyone waves, already knowing each other.

Holleen spends the majority of time talking and laughing with the moms, and Bart spends more time talking and laughing with the children.

Gaining their trust.

Because if a kid likes someone, the mom is more willing to let the person in too. Especially a kindly old man like Bart. Plus, getting to know the kid gives insight into the family and their habits.

No, it's not the mom Bart zeros in on, it's the kid. Given this pattern, then Bart one time had to know Marji.

Holleen Ickert, have you always been involved? She's in the same age range as Mom and Marji, so it is plausible. Bart began his killing spree forty years ago. Did Holleen know my mom and Marji? Was she their friend? Did she play with them?

Probably so.

A good hour or so goes by while the group meets and walks around the mall. They do various things: eating, coffee, video games, shopping... And the whole time Bart Novak grins, laughs, and comes across as the most attentive grandfather-type figure there is.

Eventually, the time comes to an end and the group disperses. Bart and Holleen casually make their way back to the garage, and I follow. They come to a stop by his car and I hover behind a cement pillar to observe.

Holleen hugs him. "I'm so glad you let me do this with you."

"Yes, well." He steps from the hug and unlocks his door.

She reaches for him. "I miss you."

"We see each other nearly every day."

"But not like this. You introduced me as your daughter in there." Tears well in her eyes.

Bart takes a patient breath. "There's a reason for that."

"What?" She takes another step. "What is the reason?"

He climbs inside the car. "Never mind that." He waves her off. "Sorry, sweetie, need to go."

Another step. "Is this about what happened in that house all those years ago?"

Bart pauses in closing his door.

Holleen lowers her voice. "I told myself it was a dream. But it wasn't, was it?"

Slowly, he climbs back out of the car. "Now slow down." With a glance around the parking lot, he pulls her in, keeping his voice down. "What are you talking about?"

"I saw you that night. Back when I was just a little girl. My friend, Marji. You went to her house. They were renting from you. That's how I met Marji. I remember. You parked outside and told me you needed to talk to her mom. You said you'd be a while and to wait in the car. You even put a blanket over me in case I got cold.

But after fifteen minutes, I got out and I went up to her house. Her mom was pleading, 'No, no please'. I saw you hand her a knife. You said, 'But if you don't do this, I'll kill your daughter and I'll do it while you watch.'

I saw Marji sleeping on the couch. You walked over to her. You taunted her with the blade. 'What did you give her?' Her mom sobbed. You said, 'A mild sedative. She'll be fine. *If* you do what you're told. She'll wake up very much alive to find you dead.'

You pushed the blade closer. 'There, there,' you said. And her hand shook as she took the knife from you, lifted it to her neck, and sliced in." Holleen catches her breath. "There was so much blood."

Bart steps toward her, grasping her upper arms. "None of that is true. It was a horrible nightmare."

She shakes her head. "No, it wasn't. When it happened again in the same house, I knew it. I did a little digging and found out your mother, my grandmother, tried to commit suicide like that." Holleen places her palms on his chest. "Daddy, you were there. I remember."

Bart's fingers dig into her arms even more and Holleen flinches. "No, you're wrong."

"It's okay," she says. "I'll protect your secret. You didn't mean it. It was just that one time."

His knuckles pop white he squeezes her arms so hard. "You will stay out of my business. Do you understand me, young lady?"

Her hopeful expression shifts to desperation. "Wait. No—"

"In fact, you're officially on restriction. I don't want to see you. I don't want to talk to you. Nothing." He lets go and she stumbles back.

"Daddy—"

He holds up a finger. "You're a stupid girl. I don't know why I bothered reconnecting with you and coming back here."

"No! I'd do anything for you. I love you, Daddy!"

"You're not my problem anymore. I've changed my mind. You're not on restriction. You're on your own. Do you hear me? I don't want you in my life."

She reaches for him. "No, please. Mom's gone, and you're all I have."

"The same does not apply. In fact, I'm sorry you were ever born. The world would be a lot better without you in it."

"No!" She cries and he ignores her as he gets in his car, cranks his engine, and drives off.

Holleen stands there crying, watching him go. The woman is in her forties and being put on restriction by her daddy? What a mess. But that last part with him cutting her off completely? From her reaction, I'd say those words officially broke her.

In an off-putting way, one tiny part of me wants to comfort her. Three girls saw the murder that night. Holleen and my mom saw it as it was happening. Marji woke up to see the aftermath. Then she hid in the closet with my mom and together they stared at the bloody mess until my grandmother arrived the following morning.

Three girls. Three paths.

Holleen apparently spent her life talking herself in and out of what happened, always wanting but never quite getting her father's love and approval.

Three girls. Three paths.

Mom and Marji went on to become killers. Which leads me to the question: if Mom wouldn't have been in that closet, then Marji would have never hid. Marji would have run for help just like every other kid did. Because of Mom, though, she hid in that closet and they were surrounded by death for an entire night. They stared at the blood and aftermath. They smelled it. They felt the energy of the kill in the air.

I was right. He doesn't actually do the kill. He makes the mother take her own life.

Yes, one tiny part of me wants to comfort Holleen. But the bigger part doesn't want me to lose Bart, and so I climb in my Jeep and race through the garage. Luckily a line of cars stall him, and I catch up with him at the EXIT.

Back in traffic, I continue to follow, merging onto the interstate. From inside my glove box, the burner phone that I purchased rings. The only people I gave that number to live and work at Aveda.

"Yes?" I answer.

Bart speaks, "Maggie, I saw you at the mall. You're snooping. I don't appreciate that."

"What were you doing with all those moms and kids?" I don't bother denying it.

"I don't know what you think you know, but I promise you, you're wrong."

"Why don't we meet somewhere? We can talk through things." And I can finally kill you.

Bart chuckles. "Not today, Maggie Caine. Not today."

He hangs up.

Up ahead his car picks up pace, swerving, and cuts off down a ramp. All around horns go off. I whip my wheel right, trying to follow, but it all happens too quickly and the exit zooms by.

"Dammit!" I bang my steering wheel. The next off-ramp sits a half mile up. Even if I double back, there's no way to find him. Not now.

This is on me. I let this go on too long.

So I do the only thing I can. I drive to Aveda Home and I wait for Mr. Novak to return.

53

One hour bleeds into another, and another, then another. Bart Novak never returns. I'm about to give up when I spy his daughter walking across the parking lot toward Aveda's front door.

I'm out of my Jeep and across the lot before she steps on the sensor that opens the door. "Holleen."

She stops walking and turns to look at me. "Wh-what are you doing here?"

I look down to her upper arm where Bart squeezed too tightly. She's wearing a coat but I would guess there's a nice bruise there now. With caution, she looks around the dark lot, I'm sure curious why I'm here given the last time she saw me I had delivered a rib-shot to Bart on behalf of the dog.

"Look," I say. "I need to find your dad."

Fiddling with her purse strap, she frowns.

"We both know what he's capable of."

Holleen's face pales. "I don't know anything."

"He'll never know you helped me." I take a step closer, lowering my voice. "He hurt you." I touch her bicep, and she flinches. "Has been hurting you, emotionally *and* physically."

She steps away from my touch.

"There's a big ugly world out there," I say. "And you can help put an end to at least some of it. Can I ask you something?"

Her feet shuffle nervously from side-to-side. "O-okay."

"How many people know that you're his daughter?"

"No one."

"Why keep you a secret?"

"B-because it's what he thinks is best."

I let a few beats go by. "You would be doing the right thing to tell me what you know. Where would he be?"

"How come you're the only one who can see my dad for what he is?"

Let's just say we have things in common.

"Who are you? You're not a cop, are you?"

I look older than eighteen and so it's a common misconception. "Yes, something like that."

Holleen looks down at her dress boots. "I wish Mom were still here," she mumbles. "She passed away five years ago now."

"Is that who raised you, your mom?"

"Yes." Holleen sighs. "I really don't know much about my father."

I lean in. "You know more than you should."

She steps around me, finally heading inside Aveda. I follow. At this time of night, no one occupies the lobby. I wait patiently while the current desk clerk gets up and signs out and Holleen takes her place.

She was working earlier and now again tonight. Two shifts in one day. A hard worker. A nice woman. She deserves better than Bart for a father.

After she's settled, she glances up, spies me, and sighs.

I lay all my cards on the table. "I heard you in the garage talking to Bart a few hours ago at the mall. Your childhood friend, Marji. You saw her mother kill herself. It wasn't a nightmare. It really happened. What you don't know is that there were many more."

She doesn't move. Carefully, I eye her expression. She's either good at masking or is truly in the dark about his annual kills. I vote the latter. Though she's not in the dark about the one she witnessed. Either way, she knows her father is not a good man.

Turning from me, she types a password into the computer. "I don't know what you're talking about."

"You sure about that? You've suspected all along that something was off. But I get it. He's your father. You want to think the best."

"I love my father."

Grasping the counter, I lean in. "I don't doubt that, but your father is a killer."

"If you don't get out of here, I'm calling the cops. Because I don't think you are one." She lifts her green gaze that matches Bart's. I hope that's the only thing she inherited from him. For the first time, I detect fire in her eyes and not the compliant woman she usually portrays.

I take a step back from the counter, purposefully backing down. "I get it. He's your dad. You're protecting him. I would do the same for my parent. I don't know my dad but my mom and I were close, too." I glance away, really working the emotion. "Actually, no we weren't. I wanted us to be, but she never quite noticed me, ya know?"

The fire in her eyes dims a little. "And you were always hungry for her approval."

I sigh. "Well, when you say it like that it makes me sound weak."

Holleen digests that. "I really don't want to talk about our parent approval issues."

"Fine but know that you can do the right thing. Somewhere along the way, I realized my mom wasn't who I thought she was. Then it didn't matter what she thought of me anymore because I didn't think much of her either."

She considers those words.

"Just tell me where you think he is," I try again.

"I've tried to be a good daughter." She shakes her head. "The best. I wanted his love. That's all." She huffs an unamused laugh. "But he hates me. He doesn't love me. He hates me." Tears fill her eyes. "He's a killer."

I nod. "Yes."

"I saw what he did all those years ago."

"But those are his choices, not yours. You can do something positive out of this." I lean in again. "Tell me where you think he is."

Her eyes cloud over. "How many other people has he killed?"

"A lot."

Something shifts in her, a denial that gradually transforms into acceptance. Realization. A knowing that her father is an evil man.

With a sniff, she uses a tissue to wipe her nose. "There's an old boat yard down by the Potomac that he often times visits when he wants to think. He might be there."

Of course. He's a creature of habit. He'll revisit the spot where his mother finally ended her life. "Thank you." Reaching over the counter, I grasp her hand in an out-of-character move for me. "Your father was wrong about something."

"What's that?" she whispers.

"This world is a better place with you in it. Don't you ever let him or anyone tell you otherwise." I squeeze her hand. "Okay?"

With a nod, she disengages our hands and pushes back from the desk. "I need a few minutes," she says and walks off.

I want to follow, but instead, I stay right where I am. She's a decent woman and has been nothing but kind and generous with me each time I've come here. I hope she heard me. I don't want Bart getting inside of her head.

54

At the boatyard, I park in the shadows and quietly climb from my Jeep. As I step through the darkness, music filters through the air. Something old that I don't recognize, scratchy as if it was taken from a record and placed onto a CD.

The music comes from a white four-door, and in front of it, Bart slow-dances to the tunes with his mother's pillow held to his chest. That's not his car. He drives a beige Corolla. "This was her favorite song," he says.

I step from between two dry-docked boats and into the moonlight. "Was it?"

He keeps dancing, his eyes closed, a pleasant curve on his lips. "It wasn't my fault."

"No," I agree. "Your mother's suicide was not your fault." Everything else though? Yes, very much his fault.

"How is it you know who I am?"

I lay all my cards out. He should know the truth before I kill him. "Forty years ago you forced a woman to slit her throat. Her daughter, Marji, was asleep on the couch. What you didn't know is that my mother saw the whole thing. She was hiding in the closet."

"And yet she wasn't able to give a good enough description of me to the cops." He clicks his tongue.

"She was five. She was traumatized. Scared for her life. When Marji woke up and found her mother bled out, she joined my mom in the closet. They stayed there all night with the blood and gore."

"And where are they now?" He keeps slow dancing.

"Don't worry, they're both dead." I smirk. "I'm the only one alive who knows who you really are."

"Ah, I see." He opens one eye. "Maggie Cain, do you like chocolates?"

"Yes."

He nods over to the hood of the car and to where a tin of chocolates sit. One piece beside it is partially eaten. "Do you want some?"

This is how he does it. He gets the kid and possibly the mom to eat those chocolates tainted with a sedative. They both pass out. She wakes up first. By then he's transported them both to the kill spot. He forces the mom to kill herself. The kid then wakes up to find the mom dead.

Jesus.

Wait a minute, a piece partially eaten.

I look around the dark boatyard and the surrounding ground, and my heart lurches. A small body lays curled up in the winter grass. No, no it's too soon. Bart isn't supposed to kill until next November.

This is on me. I set this off. My snooping triggered his cycle early.

Which means the mom is around here, too. "Where is she?" I take a step closer. "Where's the mom?"

Bart walks over and lays the pillow on the hood next to

the chocolates. "Walk away, Maggie. None of this concerns you."

Another step closer. "You know I can't do that."

Bart lunges, hurling the chocolates at me, and I duck and dodge as he lunges again. He throws a punch that catches air. I whirl around, landing a side kick into what should be his knee but lands on his thigh instead.

He stumbles, rounding the hood of the car and I brace myself for what he's going to throw next, but he doesn't.

Instead, he grabs the pillow and races through the night toward the trees.

I don't chase. There's a drugged and unconscious boy that is more important right now, and a mom that I need to find.

From inside the trunk, someone bangs. "Help me!" a woman screams.

Oh, thank God, she's alive.

Leaving her there, I race across the dried grass and come down on my knees next to the boy. I recognize him. He's from the Mommy and Me group from earlier today.

I slip one glove off and touch my fingers to his neck, and I breathe out when a strong and solid pulse flutters my skin.

Slipping my glove back on, I pat him down and find a phone in his coat pocket. I dial 911 and leave it right there by his head.

As I hightail back to my Jeep, I scan the area. I have no clue if Bart is watching, but I'll wait here in the shadows until rescue arrives.

I wish there was another way, but as of now, everyone will know Bart Novak's name. They'll know he abducted this mom and son and drugged them. As of a few minutes from now, he'll be on every radar.

Which means I need to find him first.

55

"Police aren't sure what the kidnapper had planned, but thanks to the boy dialing 911 before passing out, both mother and son were found safe. Although there are no leads as to who the abductor was, authorities say they will continue their investigation."

This is what filters over my radio early the next morning as I drive to my Patch and Paw shift. Which means the mother and boy didn't remember Bart Novak giving them tainted chocolate or they did and local law is keeping that under wraps.

Depending on the sedative used, though, there would be temporary memory loss.

My burner phone rings. That has to be Bart. "Yes?"

"What kind of person witnesses an abduction and doesn't report it?" Bart asks.

"How do you get the mom to do it?" I counter. "You threaten the kid's life, but who's to say you won't kill the kid, too?"

He chuckles. "News clippings from years gone by—a little bit of proof is all they need."

"You think you're so clever."

"Who are you, Maggie Cain? What do you want?"

"A simple one-on-one, that's all. You and me in a private place to talk." A private place to end this and you.

"Talk, hm?"

He knows I don't want to just talk. "We either meet somewhere, or I'll tell the cops who you are."

"That's not possible. I'm not even in the area anymore."

Bull shit. "Where are you?"

Another chuckle. "Like I'd tell you."

"You have 24 hours to get back into town. Clock starts now." With that, I click off.

Coming to a stop at a red light, I look across the intersection to Whole Foods, where Tommy works. I have time to spare before my shift and so I turn on my blinker and pull in.

He should be stocking produce so I round the aisle in that direction to find him standing dressed in a green apron talking to a pretty brunette. Not stocking produce.

He says something. She laughs.

He says something else. She playfully pushes his shoulder.

He chuckles at that. She flips her hair.

I don't know who this chick is but she's in full-on flirting mood, and from Tommy's posture, he's not exactly fending her off.

He glances up then, and to his credit, he doesn't do one of those I've-just-been-busted-flirting-with-another-girl-by-my-girlfriend moves. Instead, he grins and waves.

Okay, that's a good reaction.

With a few parting words to the girl, he steps around her, weaving his way through the produce section, doesn't even say hi, and instead pulls me in for warm hug followed by an equally warm kiss.

He steps back. "Did I know you were coming?"

The girl is now "shopping" for avocado all while keeping us in her peripheral. "I was passing by and figured I'd say hi."

He follows my line of sight back to the girl.

"New friend?" I ask.

"Not really. Her brother works here, so she stops by every now and again." Tommy turns back to me, studying my face. "Lane Cameron, are you jealous?"

"No." I scoff. "Of course not." I shrug. "Though you were kind of flirting."

Tommy's lips twitch. "I'm sorry."

"Apology accepted."

He moves in for another snuggle. "Are you sure? Maybe we need to kiss and make up."

Playfully, I shrug. "I guess I can put it all behind me. Move on."

"I don't know. If I were you—" his tongue flitters across my earlobe— "I'd be hurt—" his lips graze my skin— "angry—" his hot breath warms my neck— "mean even." He uses his teeth and everything in me goes from warm to full-on fire.

"Is that how you want me to feel?" I breathe.

Over the loudspeaker a man says his name. With one last bite that's just a little painful, good painful, he steps back. "Later."

I enjoy a few seconds of his excellent ass strolling away before turning to flirty girl who is still at the avocados as she watches Tommy's ass too.

Let it go. Walk out. Be on my way. Yeah, none of those are in my nature. So I walk through produce straight to her.

In every way, she is the exact opposite of me: petite, curvy, brunette, all happy.

Coming to a stop beside her, I look down into her pretty face. "Hello."

She jumps back. "Oh my God! You scared the crap out of me."

My smile is tight when I say, "Stop flirting with my boyfriend."

Nervous laugh. Flip of hair. "I wasn't flirt—"

"Yes, you were and don't lie. It's rude."

Her mouth opens. Closes. Opens.

Reaching past her I select an avocado and hand it to her. "Here."

She takes it, holding it out like it's a grenade instead of produce.

I turn her toward the register. "Now, let's get that thing bought and then I'll see you to your car. Sound good?"

"Y-yes."

My fingers dig into her shoulder just a little too firmly. "Good."

56

After my Patch and Paw shift, I swing home to grab a quick bite. I walk in our house, grab the remote, and turn on the TV. As local news flickers on, I strip out of my jacket and head into the kitchen to assemble a turkey and Swiss sandwich.

A reporter says, "The assailant broke into her studio apartment, didn't take a single thing, and cut her throat to leave her bleeding out in her kitchen. If anyone has any information on Maggie Cain's murder, please call..."

My head snaps up. Son of a bitch. Bart Novak is not out of town. He is very much local and looking for me. Because of me, that girl, Maggie Cain, is dead.

Leaving the sandwich right where it is, I run upstairs and grab Daisy's MacBook. I launch the white pages and look for any more Maggie Cains in the surrounding area. Luckily, there are none.

One thing's for sure, Bart now knows I'm not Maggie Cain.

Her death is on me. This is my fault.

I tucked the burner phone into my back pocket and it rings now as I'm racing back downstairs. I answer, "Bart."

"I went looking for you. Imagine my surprise when the girl who walked into the apartment wasn't you." He tisks. "A big disappointment."

Silently, I come down the last few steps and move into the dining room and over to the blinds. I inch them open and peer out but see only the usual neighborhood cars.

Bart says, "Then I checked the volunteer application at Aveda. Yet another surprise to find your home address as my childhood home. This tells me that you've been lying to me since the day we met."

Yep, that about covers it. "Well, in the big scheme of things, lying isn't so bad. I mean compared to the fact you spent the past forty years killing innocent women."

"I didn't kill them! They killed themselves!"

A smirk crawls across my lips. Looks like I hit a trigger point. "So given you're really in town. Are you ready to meet?"

"Why should I trust that you just want to meet and talk?"

"Because I'm holding the cards. All I have to do is go to the cops with my eye witness testimony and there will be an all-out manhunt for you. Is that what you want?"

"Tomorrow. Let's meet tomorrow."

"Fine. Noon at 'our' address." With that, I click off.

Perfect, I'll go to my morning class, kill Bart Novak over lunch, and be early for my Patch and Paw shift.

Organization. Lists. Just thinking it through already makes me feel better.

Bart Novak is unfinished business.

I dial Aveda, wanting to check on Holleen. If Bart went

there to research my volunteer application then they likely came across each other.

"Aveda Retirement, this is Edith. May I help you?"

"This is Maggie Cain, one of the volunteers. I was hoping to talk to Holleen Ickert. Is she there?"

"I'm sorry, Maggie." Edith clears her throat. "Holleen was found in Mr. Novak's room last night. Drug overdose in an apparent suicide."

Anger, tangible and pure, flares through me and keeps me from articulating a response. A real suicide or one induced by her father? My gut says by her father.

His own daughter is now dead. Because of him. He told her this world would be better off without her, and she listened. He probably handed her the pills and she took them.

Or is this on me? The real Maggie Cain is dead because of me. That mother and child, though still alive, were abducted because of me. And now Holleen is dead.

Why didn't I kill him when I had a chance in the woods or in the house when he made a suicide pact with me? Because of my morbid curiosity, innocent people have suffered.

This isn't me, and I'm ashamed of myself. I should have never let it go on this long.

57

After my morning class, I jog to my Jeep, more than ready for this meeting with Bart. It's time to say goodbye to him and put an end to his reign of terror.

Zipping up my jacket, I weave through the sea of student vehicles, and pulling out my Jeep key, I step up to the driver's door.

All around me, students pulling in, getting out, and others leaving. Very normal and usual with no one aware I'm about to kill a madman.

I open my door. In the side mirror a shadow shifts and moves. I turn right as a person steps between my Jeep and the car parked beside me.

My body sways and my hand comes out to grasp the open door.

Bart smiles. "Hello, Lane Cameron."

He knows my name. He knows I'm a student. He probably knows where I work. My family.

My family.

What the hell have I done? "How did you find me?"

"I have my ways."

Meaning, he likely followed me. I swallow. "Not here. We should talk somewhere else."

From behind his thick glasses, his eyes crinkle in amusement. "So you can what, exact justice? What do you want, Lane Cameron?"

"I want you out of my life."

"I could care less about your life." He leans in. "If I were you, I'd give up this vigilante thing. You're not very good at it." Still, with amused eyes, he turns away. "See you around, Lane Cameron."

He strolls through the parking lot, smiling at a few students, out for a merry little day.

He's right. I screwed up. I let it come to this. But no more.

Jumping in my Jeep and chasing him is an option, but my family sits at the forefront of my mind. Does he know where we live? Has he been by our home?

I don't want to lead Bart to them. I should call Victor, but what exactly am I going to say? There's a serial killer that is possibly after you all? I would then have to lay the whole thing out. He would then call in the FBI. An all-out manhunt ensues. Bart once again falls off the radar. My family will forever be in danger until he's found.

No.

But I do want them safe and out of town. Daisy is my best bet. I check my watch. She's at school right now and it's lunchtime. She'll answer.

One ring hasn't even completed by the time she picks up. "Everything okay?"

"I'm going to ask something of you, and I don't want any questions. I want only trust. I promise I will explain later."

A beat of silence goes by. "Okay."

"It's Friday and school lets out in an hour. You don't have

a car. Walk to Justin's school and pick him up. Take a Lyft to Dad's office. Don't go home. Make it an adventure for Justin. Tell Dad you want to do another weekend getaway. Spur of the moment. Fun. You'll get supplies on the road. You got it? We've talked about role-playing. This is you playing an important role."

"Lane, you're scaring me. What's going on?" Her voice breaks. "Are you okay?"

"I am absolutely fine. I promise you. You know me. I would not be calling you like this if it wasn't important."

More silence goes by. "Dad can help."

"No, Daisy. You can't tell him. Please just do as I ask. I will tell you everything after the weekend. I promise."

Yet more silence. "Will you text me? I need to know you're okay."

"I will. I'll text every two hours."

"You promise?"

"Yes, I do. And if you don't get a text from me, you can tell Dad. I just need the weekend. Then all will be okay. I'm trusting you with this, Daisy."

"Okay," she finally says. "I'll do it. But I swear, Lane, if I don't get a text from you every two hours, I'm telling Dad."

"Deal." I go to hang up when her voice filters back through the speaker.

"Tell me something I don't know," she says. "You want me to do this for you, then you tell me something I don't already know."

Tommy said a similar thing to me in the weeks following his discovery that I was related to the killer of his sister. And so I tell Daisy what I told Tommy. "When I was three I was kidnapped by The Decapitator. I was found in a house in Herndon, mute, sitting on a blood-soaked bed, holding the hand of a woman that The Decapitator had mutilated."

Daisy gasps. "Oh my God. Lane..."

"It's okay. I've known a while now and have dealt with it."

"Did Mom know? Does Dad? Jesus, this is a lot to take in."

"Mom knew and though Dad has never said, I assume so. They were married when it happened. Dad probably holds out hope that I carry no memories of it. He's just trying to protect me." I follow that with, "Explains a lot about me, huh?"

"That's not funny. You turned out really damn well and don't ever question that. You hear me, big sister?"

A smile works its way into my lips. "I hear you."

She blows out a breath. "Now what the hell am I supposed to do with all of that?"

"You keep it to yourself and you get Dad and Justin out of town. I'll text every two hours. I promise."

"I love you, Lane. Without you, I don't know what I would do. I can't lose you."

"You won't."

"You have your demons, we both do, but we don't have to be a slave to them."

My sister, the wise one. "I wish that were true."

"It is. We wouldn't be who we are without each other. You've supported me and taught me how to have confidence. We are the constant good things in each other's lives. Always remember that," she says. "You can conquer whatever darkness those demons bring."

"Then that goes for you, too. I love you, Daisy. I've got to go. Every two hours. I promise." I hang up, feeling lighter than I have in quite a while. I was right to share that with Daisy, and she accepted it as I always hoped she would.

She'll get Victor and Justin out of town. She won't let me down.

My family is in this mess because of Bart Novak.

Wrong. They're in this mess because of me. I should have taken care of him when I had a chance.

If Victor gets involved, the FBI will eventually find Bart. But I don't want that. I have to be the one to end this. I have to know he's gone forever. For my family. For me.

I wasn't thinking clearly before. I got sidetracked. Because of my mother's connection to all of this. Even dead, she's controlling my life. But it is my life, like it or not.

Yes, I am in control. Not Bart. Not my evil family legacy.

I am.

Sometimes, though, I'm just going along and everything makes sense and then this darkness creeps in and takes over. It makes me both focused and irrational at the same time.

How is that even possible?

58

As I'm putting my Jeep in gear, about to drive from the student lot, I remember the burner phone. I fish it out of my backpack and the second I plug it in to charge, the phone chimes with an email to the fake Maggie Cain account that I set up. I put the Jeep back in park and pull it up.

It's from Holleen, time-stamped last night. Given that she's dead, she either put a delayed delivery on this or my damn phone battery died.

I touch my finger to the flag and find no message, only an audio file attached. I press play.

"Daddy! What are you doing?"

"I need whatever you've got. Jewelry, cash, anything of value."

"What's going on?"

"Now, Holleen. Now!" He snaps.

Rustling filters through the speakers as Holleen gathers whatever she can find. Where are they? Her house?

"Give me that ring," he orders.

"Ow!" She yelps. "Stop pulling on me. No, this belonged to Momma."

"I don't care. This is it? Stop pretending you don't have things. I need more. How much do you have in the bank?"

"Daddy, just tell me what's happening?"

A slap resonates through the speakers and I cringe. "Do not ever question me!" Bart yells. "Someone very bad is after me."

Holleen cries. "Where are you going?"

"To take care of my problem." Something rattles. "Here."

"What are these?"

"Pills to take care of *your* problem. I said the world would be better off without you, and I meant it."

The sound of a door slamming echoes through the speaker followed by Holleen's voice, "Maggie, this is Holleen. He's coming for you. Run. Do you hear me? Run!"

The audio file clicks off and I release a breath. She went to Aveda after this, let herself into his room, and took the pills. Perhaps she wanted to die surrounded by his things. Or she hoped he would find her. Who knows? But goddamn it, if I'd only received this last night I would have stopped her before she took those pills.

I throw the phone down and put my Jeep in reverse. Bart abandoned her, but the damage was already done. He'd crawled so far inside of her head there was no going back. He killed his own daughter and so many others.

I would never abandon my family.

But is that ultimately how to save them? Is leaving them better than staying? Are they safer with me out of their lives?

Because of me a very dangerous man now knows I have a family. If he knows my name, then he knows theirs, too. Sooner or later history will repeat and another madman will threaten my family. They will eventually pay for who I've become. I always thought they'd eventually pay for Mom's real identity, but it'll be me. It won't be her that they have branded across their forehead, it'll be me.

Lane, the killer.

We are the constant good things in each other's lives.

No one, especially Holleen, can say that about Bart. So maybe I'm wrong. Things might turn out differently for me and my family.

For now, though, they are safe and I'm pretty damn sure where Bart is headed.

59

Whon comfortable, Bart Novak is a creature of habit. When backed into a corner, he's a feral cat on the attack.

He won't leave this area without loose ends tied, knotted, and burned.

And I'm a loose end that has backed him into one hell of a corner. He told Holleen he was going to "take care of a problem". Clearly, I am that problem.

Then he'll be leaving town with all the things he pillaged from his daughter.

Or at least that's what he thinks.

With my fingers twined tight around the wheel, I drive. I had a whole lot of fun with the animal control pole I used months ago on Mr. Oily Nose, the pedophile. But I promised myself I would use Bart's method. He needs to experience what he does to others.

Something icy pokes around in my guts, like prodding fingers urging me toward this wonderful ending. I should have listened to that prodding earlier.

As I near our neighborhood, my breath turns momentarily shaky, and it shames me. Where's the control? Perhaps if I'd moved earlier on the Suicide Killer it would be here in full force and void of the shake.

I take a long and deep breath to steady myself, and I survey every car in our community. No Bart. That's not to say he isn't here.

He drives a beige Corolla. He also had a white four-door when he took that mother and child. There's no telling what he's in now.

Knowing Victor is gone, I push the remote on my visor and pull into his spot in the garage. I'll be inside waiting when Bart arrives.

The garage door goes back down and whispers whirl and swell through my head. Music.

He's here. And he knows I'm here, too.

The icy poking that was in my guts turns to fire. It flames through my veins. I'm on my own turf. I have the upper hand.

From the glovebox, I take the sedative that I stole from Patch and Paw and load a syringe. Bart uses a sedative, and so will I. Then I'll take him to the old boat yard and hang him from a tree in a perfect ending to his morose excuse of a life.

With the syringe tucked securely in my back pocket, I grip my bokken and I slip silently from the Jeep. Through the garage, I cat-step, up the two steps, and slide into our house. The music comes louder now, the same old piece he listened to before.

I slide carefully across the laundry room, focused on the open door that leads into the great room. Faint afternoon light filters in from the closed blinds and I stalk further in. My fingers tighten around the bokken. My senses prick.

From where I stand hovering at the doorway that leads

from the laundry room into the main room, I see a shadow shift, drawing my attention to the right. With his eyes closed and holding the pillow tight to his chest, Bart dances to the music coming from his phone.

I don't move as he shuffles in a box-step in the tiny area between the coffee table and the couch. And the more I watch, the more intrigued I become. He's not scared to be here. In fact, he doesn't appear to care I just walked in. But he knows I'm here.

His music slows, coming to a stop. He halts dancing.

Still, I don't move. "Hello, Bart."

He opens his eyes. "You were picturing a different scenario, no?"

True, I was. "You're a special kind of evil, aren't you?"

His eyes brighten. "Do tell."

I can't believe I actually thought I could learn something from this man. And now he thinks I've complimented him.

"You think you're so clever figuring me out." He hugs the pillow closer. "You have a little monster inside of you and you can't control it any more than I can mine."

"You never even tried."

"Oh, I tried, but what's the point? It's better to embrace who you are."

"So what's your desirable ending here, Bart? You'll do me and then disappear to someplace new? That's naïve."

He shrugs. "I don't have a family. I can do what I want." He looks over at the mantel where several framed photos sit. "But you have a family. Just look at them." He takes two steps to the side, leaning over to pick one up.

"Don't touch those." I move forward, taking the step that shifts me from the laundry room into the great room. My toe snags on a clear plastic line and I trip forward, coming down hard on my hands and knees.

He moves quickly, and before I have a chance to react, he's right beside me. Something pricks my neck, stinging and tingling, and I glance up to see Bart staring down at me through thick glasses.

My body weight shifts. The room floats. And all the bones in my limbs melt me to the floor.

I'm stalking merrily along, trailing a very bad person. But then my feet become heavy and I'm no longer merry as I drag them through the mud. I wobble, reaching over my shoulder for the bokken strapped to my back, but it's not a bokken, it's a lightsaber.

Lightsaber?

Pain slices through me and now my arm is severed from my body. By me. I'm cutting it with the lightsaber. My skin burns. I hit an artery and red spews out and up to cover my face and blind me.

I'm falling, falling, falling into a dark abyss. Awful shapes fill the void—twisted and distorted images of dead people. They bump into me. Bounce off of me. Get away! Get away!

Open your eyes.

A sharp odor knifes up my nostrils.

With a flinch, I force my lids to open and my world comes back into focus. Thick lenses greet me, and green eyes. A balding head, and the average height and chubby middle of Bart Novak.

"There you are." He holds up a tiny plastic vial. "Smelling salts."

My nostrils burn and leak fluid. My thick tongue sticks to the roof of my mouth. I dig in my brain for any memory of what happened. I was on campus, right?

This is what the kids must feel like when they wake up. Disoriented. Unable to grasp where they were last. Except they don't see Bart Novak, they see their dead mother, and it sends them into an emotional spiral.

Deep inside my brain a fierce monster roars and it's the only reason why I don't flinch away or struggle. I try to move my hands and feet but can't. He's tied and taped me up.

Bart blinks at me. "Can you hear me? I've never stayed around to see someone wake up." Delight touches his voice. "This is neat."

I continue to struggle to piece together the events. One thing is for sure—I'm dumb to have walked into this. My own curiosity and carelessness put me here.

He straightens up a little, and his smile turns to a gloating smirk.

I'm lying on our couch. And he's sitting directly in front of me on our coffee table. I have to say something. He can't think I'm afraid.

I pull my tongue from the roof of my mouth and it clicks into place. I concentrate hard on my words. Too hard, but I don't want to appear disoriented. "We're in my home," I speak. "A home that will soon have people walking in."

Something buried in a crevice of my memory tells me that's not an accurate statement. Why isn't my brain working? How long until it does?

That gloating smirk inches up. "Then we'll need to make the best of this." He leans in. "But I assure you. I can take care of myself. I also work quickly."

I underestimated this old man, and if the drugs weren't making me so dopey, I might figure a way out of this.

"I'm curious." He folds his arms. "If you knew who I was all along, why didn't you do something about it?"

The truth comes out of my mouth, but I don't want it to. "Because I wanted to observe you. Study you." Clearly, a mistake.

He chuckles. "And are you regretting this decision?"

I don't answer him because yes, I am, but I won't give him any more fuel.

Bart pats my shoulder. "That's okay, you don't have to answer every question, just some."

On the coffee table sits his leather zipper pouch open in a not-so-cheerful image. Lined up are his kill weapons— scalpel, pills, a noose.

He stares at me, his eyes huge behind those thick lenses. "Lane Cameron, which do you choose? Or shall I choose for you?"

"How wonderful that you think I'll commit suicide." I'm glad to have a bit of snark back.

Bart frowns. "Oh, no. Sorry. I'm actually going to do you. You'll be my second. Maggie Cain was the first." He purses his lips. "You should be more frightened. Why aren't you scared and begging?"

Because I'm not giving him the satisfaction.

He pushes up off the coffee table, moving away, and giving me a chance to focus on me. I lay sideways on the L-shaped couch with the coffee table and the front door all within my line of sight. To the left sits the laundry room and beyond that the garage. To the right our kitchen and the stairwells—one up to the second floor and one down to the basement.

The laundry room. The garage. That's right. I tripped over a line he strung up.

I put more effort into moving my arms and legs, glad to be gaining my focus back, but he's secured them with duct tape and connected them behind my back like I'm a calf he's wrangled in a rodeo.

Humming, he makes his way into the kitchen. I can't see what's he's doing, but from the slight suction sound of the refrigerator being opened, it sounds like he's making himself at home. He's taking his time with me.

Wait, my family won't be coming home. I told Daisy to get Victor and Justin out of town. Does Bart somehow know this?

Piece by piece more fog clears from my brain. How long have I been unconscious? I told Daisy I would text every two hours.

Oh, no...has it been two hours?

I lift my head off the cushion, trying to see the blinds and if it's day or night, but I can't tell. He's pulled the curtains *and* the blinds.

In the kitchen, the microwave goes on. Son of a bitch is making food. I tug harder on my restraints, but they don't budge. My gaze drifts back to the coffee table and to his array of instruments. Maggie Cain bled out. Holleen Ickert took a mouthful of pills. He's not giving me a choice. That noose is for me.

My throat constricts and a strangled noise wants to come out, but I swallow and keep it in. I won't let him know I'm scared. Because now that more of the chemicals have seeped from my brain, a new one trickles in—fear.

I don't care for Victor's dad, my grandfather, but right now his words come back to me: *Even in the worst of times, we have our memories to cheer us.*

Here I lay helpless, able only to hear the Suicide Killer in the kitchen and visualize the dreadful things to come. Even so, I have memories.

Like playing G. I. Joe with Justin in the yard. And that time years ago when Daisy braided my hair. When Victor and I skateboarded down the street. And that time Reggie and I sat out all night at summer camp and counted stars.

"Well," Bart says, squatting down beside me. "Doesn't look as if that family of yours is coming back."

"Making yourself at home in our kitchen? Did you make a snack?"

He cocks his head to one side and the tip of his tongue flicks out to wet the corner of his mouth. He stares at me, his eyes large and unblinking. "You're a curious thing." He pats the top of my head. "I don't think you really believe this is happening. The drugs need to leave your system. You really should be more afraid."

"Afraid of what? You?" Mom sure was. Marji, too. Or perhaps it was more they were traumatized. What would they think to know I was bantering with the very villain who shaped their lives?

Bart stares at me for a very long moment before shaking his head. "Well, Lane. I see we have our work cut out for us." He leans in, his face a tiny inch from mine.

A black shadow rears within me, clambering to meet the challenge. I don't move. I don't blink. For a moment we face off, his breath coming out hot and scented with pickles. Then he blinks, just once, and pushes away.

He walks back into the kitchen, probably to finish that pickle, and I sink into the couch. What miracle will I come up with to get out of this?

Of course, there's the two-hour text rule with Daisy, but right now that's more worrisome than anything else. Victor would note the curtains drawn. He'd know something was up. He wouldn't wait for help, he'd come charging in. But Bart would be ready and then my little couch becomes crowded with me and Victor both taped up and drugged.

Daisy, of course, would repeat the pattern. Then all three of us would be here.

Justin would be the only logical one to go for help. But by then we'll all be dead.

Truthfully, in spite of my bold and brave dialogue exchange, my brain still warbles a bit from the sleepy mickey. I'm doped, tied up, and all alone. The positive being I'm still alive and my family is safe.

Bart picks up his phone and launches a new song, this one old like the other, but softer. The gentleness of it takes me down a philosophical path. I've never put much thought into how I'll eventually die but being done in by a villain that I hunt seems ironically right. Though not preferred.

No, if I had my choice of death, I'd like to go to sleep and never wake up. A peaceful way to go. What will I see when I go? Heaven? Hell? I better not see Mom and Marji.

But doesn't one need a soul to see heaven or hell? I'd begun to think I didn't have one. How could I? It's hard enough to be who I am without a soul and a conscience and the afterlife looming overhead. My charade of life will finally be over. Done. It's just as well.

What a tragic way to think.

No, of course, I have a soul and a conscience. It's what makes me different from my evil heritage. But if I had to choose, I'd prefer reincarnation. I'd come back as a dog and I'd be Corn Chip's best friend.

People would grieve if I died. Victor, Daisy, Justin. Tommy and Zach. Reggie. Dr. O'Neal and my new roommate. They all care about me. Without wanting or trying,

I've managed to pick up an entire string of emotional attachments.

How?

And why is my brain going down this route?

Bart rattles around in the kitchen, washing his dish. So thoughtful. I lift my head, looking toward the kitchen, in time to see him step around and move toward me.

"Time to move things along." He comes to a stop standing beside me, and he leans down and picks up the noose from his bag of terror. He looks up at a beam that runs the length of our ceiling and with a cheery voice says, "That looks sturdy enough."

Leaning over, he slips the noose around my neck.

61

From behind comes a soft creak, a foot on a loose floorboard. Bart spins around and Daisy lunges. With a butcher knife gripped in her right hand, she swings back and arcs forward as if she were throwing a bowling ball and not stabbing someone.

With a yell, she sinks the large blade into his stomach.

Bart sucks in a breath, taking hold of the knife, and time stands still as his jaw goes slack.

One second. Two. Three.

He stumbles, falling over the coffee table, and lands with a loud thump onto the floor.

"Lane!" Daisy screams, and it's the most beautiful sound in the world. She teeters back and forth, her head swiveling between me and a still alive Bart, knife in his gut and all. "What do I do?"

"He's not going anywhere." My jaw muscles tighten. "Cut me loose." Let me at him.

She races into the kitchen to get scissors. Bart wheezes. He moans. He rolls over onto his side, giving me his back. Don't die, you bastard. Don't die.

Daisy's back with scissors. She slips the noose from my neck and flings it aside before gently pushing me over to get at the duct tape. Everything becomes quiet and motionless as I stare at Bart's back. Even that damn music of his ceases to play.

"Is he dead?" she whispers, frantically sawing the tape.

I hope not.

"I knew something was up when I didn't get a text from you. Then I came here and saw the drawn curtains." She keeps sawing. "Damn. Damn. Damn." She saws so hard it severs my skin. I cringe.

She casts a nervous glance over her shoulder at Bart, now curled in a tight ball, his back still to us. Blood spreads out from under his body, darkening the throw rug.

"I climbed up the tree and came in my bedroom window." She keeps cutting. "Fuck, Lane, there's so much tape."

I look at the front door. "Where's Victor?"

"Still at work. He couldn't leave. I left Justin there. Because when I didn't get a text from you, I knew something was up. Then I came here and saw the curtains—" Her hands shake. "Wait, I just said all of that."

I go back to Bart, and my heart sinks. He's barely breathing now. He's going to die and it won't be by me.

One last whack and my hands come free. With my feet still taped together, I roll off the couch and crawl over to Bart. My world spins with the damn drugs still in my system. I'm going to yank that knife from his gut and pierce his heart with it.

The palms of my hands sink into his blood spreading and darkening the carpet, making it into a giant sponge.

"What are you doing?" Daisy follows. "Get away from him."

My fingers dig into his shoulder and I move him over onto his back. Blood pumps from his neck where he used the scalpel. The leather pouch still sitting on the coffee table now has only the pills. When he fell over the table he must have grabbed the scalpel. Son of a bitch.

Through hazy eyes, he looks at me and his bloody lips quiver into an arrogant smile.

Then...then he's gone.

"NO!" I yell, and I punch him. And I punch him again. No! He was supposed to die by my hand. Mine!

A huge silence fills the room. Daisy puts her hand on my shoulder and I glance up to see her staring at me, not Bart. Me.

Something crosses her pretty face, an unexplained eeriness, but as quick as it's there, it's gone.

I turn from her and all I think is, *I wanted to kill him, and he took that away from me.*

I don't think about the fact that I'm alive.

That Daisy is okay.

That she just *stabbed* a man.

No, the fact that *I* didn't kill him is all that buzzes through my head and festers in my soul.

62

I've watched bad people suffer by my hand, and at the moment of truth I looked into their eyes and we both knew they got what they deserved.

But what happens if it's someone like Holleen or the real Maggie Cain? If you don't get what you deserve? If what you deserve is something different—a family who loves you, a future, great laughter.

What if you deserve a real sister and daughter and instead you get me?

And what happens if you kill someone, defending a sister who doesn't deserve it?

Daisy is now a killer because of me. Holleen is dead because of me. The real Maggie Cain, too. I blame myself. I should have killed Bart Novak the first chance I got.

I love Daisy. It's my job to make sure nothing bad happens to her. Somewhere along the way I even convinced myself that she was lucky to have me. But now I know she's not. She trusted me, and now she's a killer.

I'm toxic. She'd be better off without me. They all would.

Lights flash, bringing me from my thoughts. In the

distance, a siren cuts through the air, all around neighbors materialize from their homes. One cop pulls in, then another, and another.

Daisy kneels in our front yard, in the exact same spot she's been since we emerged from our house. I stand a cautious distance away.

"Miss?" A cop hesitantly approaches her. "Are you hurt? Is that your blood?"

Daisy doesn't answer, just keeps staring at the blood covering her hands and upper body. Blood belonging to Bart Novak, the man she just killed because of me.

The cop reaches for her. "Miss?"

I step forward. "Leave her alone. It's not her blood or mine."

With a hesitant glance at me, the cop reaches out a hand to Daisy, and I snap, "Back the hell off."

He holds up both hands. "What happened here?"

"I did it," Daisy mumbles. "I killed them."

I take another step forward, placing my hand on my sister's head. Gently, I pull her against me. "We're not talking to anybody but our father."

I killed them. What the hell is she talking about?

The cop steps away, trailing behind first responders moving into our home. *Never make a scene*, Mom told me that once. *Keep your emotions in check.*

I never imagined I'd be thinking this, but I could use her skills right now. Her words of advice. She'd know how to handle this whole thing.

Everybody's looking. Daisy's in shock. I'm standing here covered in duct tape. We're both smeared with Bart's blood. Hell, even our neighbor is crying, though I don't know why.

A detective approaches, taking us both in. He looks at

first me and then down to Daisy. "What happened here? You said you 'killed them'. Who's them?"

"Do not answer that." Victor crosses the yard. "You want to talk to my daughters, schedule an appointment."

With a nod, the detective turns away and Victor comes down in front of Daisy. "Sweetheart? Can you hear me? Are you hurt?"

Daisy's lips tremble. "He was going to kill Lane."

63

Victor called Gramps to come get Justin and he got us a suite at a local extended stay place. Justin has no idea what's going on. He thinks he's on a mini-vacation with his grandfather.

That was yesterday, and Daisy has barely climbed from her bed. As I stare at her, my thoughts go to the day we went to the funeral home in preparation for Mom's service...

The elderly funeral director tilts his head to the side, a sad and gentle curve to his lips. He looks across the table at me, Victor, and Daisy. "I'm sorry for your loss."

How does he do that? He sounds like he actually means it.

Victor clears his throat. "Thank you."

In his calm and low voice, the funeral director continues, "What we need to do now is make important decisions about how your wife and mother will be remembered. This is your chance to express your feelings."

"Excuse me," Daisy murmurs, pushing back from the table and leaving the office.

Victor clears his throat again, glancing at me. "Maybe I shouldn't have brought you girls."

"We wanted to come," I say. Daisy insisted on it, actually. I stand, too. "I'm going to check on her."

Victor nods, and I quietly leave the room. The funeral home and grounds are spread out and it takes me fifteen minutes to find my sister. She's outside standing near a tree, watching a memorial service currently going on.

I step up beside her. "You okay?" I whisper.

She nods across the lawn to where the people have gathered to mourn. In the front row stands a girl a little younger than us, crying. "Mom will want that, I think," Daisy says. "She'll want us crying. Isn't that what good daughters do?"

I don't answer that. I'm not a good daughter. Just like she wasn't a good mother.

"I've been looking all over for you two," Victor whispers, coming up behind us. "What are you doing?"

I turn toward him, smiling gently. "We were thinking about Mom and how much we miss her."

Daisy's eyes slide over to mine and though it's slight, I see it all over her face. She knows I don't miss Mom, and I don't think she does either. We'll pretend, though, for Justin and Victor.

I'm not sure why that memory plays in my head, but it does. Back then I didn't know the history between Mom and Daisy. My heart aches that she kept all of that to herself.

Victor's been gone all morning. The FBI released the crime scene at our house, and he went to supervise the cleanup. I offered to help and he adamantly refused.

So here I sit staring at Daisy. *I killed them.* Did I hear her right? Maybe she said "him".

With a sigh, I cross the small distance between our two beds and I pull up the white comforter from where she kicked it off to cover her curled up body. For a few seconds, I stand listening to her heavy breathing and watching her rib cage expand and contract with her slow and deep breaths.

I'm glad she's sleeping, but I also wish she'd wake up. Now that Victor's not here, I want to ask her about the "them".

Leaning forward, I lift a strand of her blonde hair that's stuck to her lips and carefully lay it on the pillow. "Thank you for saving my life," I whisper. "I don't deserve you. You're better—all of you are—without me in your lives." If only they knew who I was and what I had done. "I've led everyone to believe I'm a good sister, daughter, friend. But I'm not. It's a lie."

It's all a lie.

Turning away, I go sit back on my bed. I'll see Daisy through this and then I'm gone. There are only a few things I'll need—my Jeep, my journals, my gear. I'll start over someplace new and far away from here.

Distance will bring me clarity. It's hard to focus around my family. It's hard to breathe.

My cell buzzes with a text from Tommy: HOW YOU HOLDING UP?

OK.

DAISY?

HARD TO TELL.

JUST BE THERE FOR HER, he types.

I'M TRYING...

NEED ANYTHING?

Despite everything going on, I smile a little. I'M FINE.

JUST WANT YOU TO KNOW THAT YOU MAKE ME FEEL GOOD. I'M GLAD YOU'RE IN MY LIFE.

I don't respond. I simply stare at those words and the more I stare, the faster my heart beats.

He sends me a heart emoji that has sudden and unexpected tears coming to my eyes. What the hell?

But as quick as they come, they leave.

Tommy is another person I need to pull back from.

Everyone is better off without me.

I put my phone down and lay back on my bed. Closing my eyes, I allow my thoughts to drift. I try to make them go to Tommy and the conversation I need to have with him, but they stick instead on the day Victor told us Mom was gone.

"Something happened to Mom," Victor quietly tells the three of us.

Tears well in my brother's eyes. "Where is she? Is she okay?"

Victor looks at the three of us, sitting side-by-side on the L-shaped couch. Of course, I know what happened to Mom, but he doesn't know this. No one knows.

He paces away, stopping. He swallows, then clears his throat. His jaw clenches, and he presses his fingers into his temples.

"Dad?" Justin whispers.

I wish I could change spots with him, but I can't. I have to sit here and watch him struggle to tell us the worst news of our lives.

He breathes out, opening his eyes and turning to look at us. "I need to tell you something."

"What's going on?" Daisy asks. "You're freaking me out."

"Did something bad happen?" Justin murmurs.

The emotion Victor struggled to contain surfaces and silent tears trail from his eyes. "She was on the job hunting a killer and walked into a trap."

A rush of air leaves Daisy's lungs. "What are you saying?"

"He's saying someone killed her," I quietly speak.

Victor's wet eyes come to mine, and he nods.

"What?" Daisy lunges off the couch. "This isn't funny." She whirls on me. "Is this a joke?"

I reach for her. "Daisy."

She slaps my hand away. "Don't touch me."

"Daisy." I try again.

"I said don't touch me!" she screams.

Justin falls into me, crying. Victor slumps to kneel on the carpet, burying his face in his hands, silently weeping. Wrapping my arm around Justin, I stare up at Daisy.

Red crawls her neck to flush her face. "It doesn't even matter to you, does it?"

"Of course it does."

"No, it doesn't." She jabs a finger in my direction. "Look at you. You don't even care."

I hug Justin tighter. "I do care. I care about you, Justin, and Dad."

It happens slowly, the rage building inside of her, the quivering muscles as she tries to contain it. My gaze tracks down to her hands clenched so tight, blood splotches and strains against her fair skin. I look back into her face and I see it there, way in the depths of her eyes—a darkness I've never seen before.

I don't want to, but in this moment I find myself intrigued by Daisy. Like Mom used to be intrigued by me.

With a sigh, I come from the memory. Truthfully, with the fallout after Mom's murder and everything that's been going on, I hadn't thought of that moment.

Ever.

I had been intrigued by my sister. Curious. Maybe even titillated by her brain. An uncomfortable sensation that quickly left. Just like her. She turned and stormed from our home.

She was gone for six hours.

But between Justin's grief, and Victor, and about a dozen other things, no one focused on those six hours Daisy was missing.

I texted. Victor did, too. In the end, he said, "If she's gone eight hours, we'll go looking." He was trying to respect her space. I was as well. Yet she's never told us what she did in those six hours.

She did return at hour seven. Not angry anymore and she clearly had been drinking. I helped her to bed. In the days that followed, she remained quiet and withdrawn. Then the three of us went to the funeral home and in the weeks to follow that, my sister became very needy of my attention to the point where she slept with me nearly every night.

Since then it's been up and down with her. And just when I think I have her figured out, I don't. One day she's angry. Another she's defending Mom. Yet another she's distant. And some days she seems fine. I'm not sure I ever will figure her out.

Perhaps she feels the same way about me.

With another sigh, I open my eyes. Daisy stands right beside my bed, looking down at me.

I barely breathe. How did I not hear her get up?

"I've been thinking about us," she says, lowering to the edge of the bed.

Pulling my legs in, I push up to sit. "Oh?"

She nods. "How much I need you. Not just now, but in the days, weeks, months, and years to come." She looks down at her fingers, idly pushing the cuticle back on her thumbnail. "You'll be there for me, right?"

Was she awake this whole time? Did she hear my whispered words? "Daisy—"

She stops with the cuticle and looks me dead in the eyes. "I need to tell you something."

"Okay."

"Bart Novak wasn't the first person I killed."

64

S hit.

Shit. Shit. Shit.

I concentrate on keeping my expression accepting, supportive. "Okay, will you tell me about it?"

"Do you remember how angry I was when Dad first told us about Mom's murder?" Daisy asks.

"Yes, I was actually just thinking of that."

She looks down at her fingers again, rubbing the cuticle forward that she just pushed back. "After he told us, I left the house."

"I remember."

"I walked from our neighborhood and just kept on walking. Eventually, I got a Lyft and took it to Brentwood."

"As in Northeast D.C.?" That's the worst neighborhood in the district.

She nods. "I walked in a bar, showed my fake ID, and proceeded to drink a hell of a lot of vodka. There wasn't anybody there. Just me and the bartender. I went to the bathroom. I was hovering over the toilet and the bartender walked in. 'What's your problem?' I yelled at him. 'Get the fuck out of here!' But he didn't."

Daisy stops with the cuticle, but still, she doesn't look at me. "He locked the door. He unbuckled his belt and slid it free of the loops, all while staring at me still hovering over the toilet. 'You got a nasty mouth,' he said. 'Let's see what you can do with it'."

My hand shakes as I reach forward and grab Daisy's fingers.

"The place was dirty," she says. "Hadn't been cleaned in probably forever. He unbuttoned his jeans and unzipped them. He pulled himself out. He was already hard."

Finally, she looks up at me. Her voice lowers to a whisper. "He cracked the belt against the sink and the sound of the leather smacking porcelain echoed off the cement walls. There was a rusted pipe laying in the corner near the toilet. I grabbed it and something inside of me took over. I didn't even pull my leggings up, I lunged."

"I hit him. And I hit him again. And again. And again. I don't know how many times I hit him, but eventually, I stopped." She swallows. "There was blood everywhere. On me. Him. The bathroom walls. The grimy mirror. I dropped the pipe and I nearly busted through the door trying to get out of there. When I raced back out into the bar, I discovered he had locked the door to the bar, too. He wanted plenty of time to do whatever he wanted to do with me."

She squeezes my fingers. "So I sat there on a nasty barstool and I breathed. I calmed down. Eventually, I went behind the bar and I used the sink to clean up. I looked around and I didn't see security cameras anywhere." She lets out a harsh laugh. "Like there would be in that place. I left the front door locked and I went out the back into the alley. I walked a few blocks and I got a Lyft and I came back home. I kept waiting for a cop to show up and arrest me. But...nothing happened."

Still staring into my eyes, she swallows. "Say something."

Trembling, I pull her in for a hug, and I don't let her go. I hold her hard against me, my heart pounding in my chest. I squeeze my eyes shut, feeling her heart pounding, too. "What you did was human and right. You are not to blame. I'm proud of you. That man *deserved* your fury. Do you hear me? *Deserved* it."

My fingers dig into her shoulders as I pull back, and still trembling, I look into her frightened blue eyes. "Thank you for telling me that. I'm here for you, Daisy. Always. In the days, weeks, months, and years to come. I am here for you."

"Do you promise?"

"I do. I promise." She's not better off without me. None of them are. And I'm not better off without them.

Her bottom lip quivers. "Please don't tell anyone."

I pull her in for another hug. "I won't. This is between you and me."

She begins to cry, and I rub a hand over her back, letting her know its okay. "Listen to me, Daisy. When you're asked again, you say, you killed 'him'. Not 'them'. 'Him'. Got it?"

"Yes," she whispers. "I've got it."

65

T he story of Bart Novak comes out and fills the
news.
Or at least a version of it.

Suzie Cameron, former director of the FBI's behavioral
unit, witnessed a murder forty years ago. To protect her, her
parents chose to change their identities and relocate. Fast
forward forty years and the murderer returns to the area,
one Bart Novak, to finish what he started. Not realizing
Suzie was already dead, he tracks her to her home in
McLean, Virginia. He breaks in. He restrains her daughter,
Lane. Her other daughter, Daisy, finds them in the living
room and using a knife from their kitchen, stabs Bart Novak
in the stomach. Bart later dies from self-inflicted wounds.

That is the story that circulates the news. Some truth,
some lie.

Between Victor, Daisy, and a few high up people in the
FBI, we know the full story. The one that includes Marji
being a serial killer. The one that links Bart Novak to the
string of suicide-murders. And the one that also involves me

digging around and independently researching things as I gathered evidence to bring Bart to justice.

Justice to them meaning turning him in, but I know otherwise. Of course, Victor is irritated with me over the whole thing. But what's new?

Yes, I say they know the full story, but Mom's alter identity still stays buried deep.

. . .

Now over a week later, I sit at the dining room table, staring out the blinds and up at the half moon. My thoughts go from the past few weeks to the here and now. At this moment millions of other people see this same moon. That one piece of light connects us all.

Dark. Light.

Why do I fight against the light? I don't know. I don't need to. Yet I do. Maybe one day I'll be rid of this dark stain on my soul. Perhaps it begins with time away. Like Victor did in taking Justin and Daisy on that mini vacation. He's onto something. Life is to be lived.

I should take Daisy on a sister's weekend. It would be good for both of us.

Sliding from the chair, I move into the kitchen. A sliver of light still filters out from underneath the office door. Victor has been in there a long time.

Stepping close to the door, I pause to listen, but only silence greets me. I clear my throat. "Dad?"

But he doesn't answer.

Softly, I knock. I wait.

No answer.

I reach for the handle, swiveling it down, and I open the door.

Victor lays slouched in the leather chair, his puffy and red-rimmed eyes closed. A half bottle of whiskey sits on the desk. Logic tells me he's passed out drunk, but still, I step toward him and press my fingers to his neck.

A strong and too fast pulse flutters my skin. An alcohol pulse.

Spread on the desk under the whiskey bottle are diagrams, lists, notes, and photos of The Decapitator's killing spree. Red lines circle and connect victim names and cities—all pointing to two names in the center.

Suzie Cameron and Seth Leaf—my real parents.

Victor knows.

He stirs, mumbling, and opens his eyes. He sees what I'm looking at and moves fast to cover things up. Another photo surfaces. It's the one Reggie sent me from a long time ago when I was just three and found sitting on a blood-soaked bed holding the hand of my parents' victim.

With gentle hands, I stop Victor's frantic ones and I look down into his flushed face.

He raises tear-filled hazel eyes to mine and his lips quiver with a contained cry.

"I know," I quietly tell him.

I thought I could change who I am. But it doesn't matter. This life of mine. It's fate. "I'm the one who killed her."

OTHER BOOKS IN THIS SERIES:

The Strangler

ACKNOWLEDGMENTS

Novels do not get written in a vacuum. It is a team effort for sure! I want to first thank Patrick Price, my editor. He fell in love with Lane from the beginning and has been an ongoing cheerleader for her vigilante ways.

I'd also like to thank Steven at Novak Illustration for the excellent exterior design.

My readers, too, who are the sole reason why I write stories. Thank you for your support!

To the beta readers of *The Suicide Killer:* Sam Gutekunst, T. Lucas, and Kelsey Miller. I heart each one of you!

To Karin Perry for creating fabulous swag. You can check her store out on Zazzle under Doodle_with_Karin

Special thanks to my longtime friend, Thais Mootz, for driving me around Alexandria as we plotted out the specifics of *The Suicide Killer*.

A smile to Sabrina Klotz and Paige Akins Ulevich who pitched in on research and won a character named after them in *The Suicide Killer*. Sabrina, Lane's new roommate, and Paige, the hanging victim.

ABOUT THE AUTHOR

Things you should know about me: I write novels. Some have won awards. Others have been bestsellers. Under Shannon Greenland (my real name) you'll find spies, adventure, and romantic suspense. Under S. E. Green (my pen) you'll find dark and gritty fiction about serial killers, cults, secret societies that do bad things, and whatever else my twisted brain deems to dream up.

I'm on Instagram, Twitter, and Facebook. I can also be found at www.segreen.net. There you can sign up for my newsletter where you can keep up to date with new releases, free stuff (like books), and my mild ramblings about my travels. I have a very old and grouchy dog. But I love him. My humor runs dark and so don't be offended by something off I might say. I mean no harm. I live in a small Florida beach town but I'm most often found exploring the world. I eat entirely too many chips. I also love math!

. . .

Turn the page for a complete list of books!

BOOKS BY S. E. GREEN

Monster

When the police need to crawl inside the mind of a monster, they call Caroline. It takes a survivor to know a madman...

Vanquished

A secret island. A sadistic society. And the woman who defies all odds to bring it down.

Ultimate Sacrifice

A murdered child. A small town. A cult lurking in the shadows...

Twisted Truth Box Set

Includes four bestselling, award-winning novels. Its pages full of visceral and provocative, raw and gritty, heart-pumping, edge-of-your-seat reads.

BOOKS BY SHANNON GREENLAND

The Specialists Series
The Summer My Life Began Series

Made in the USA
Columbia, SC
06 July 2023

20121040R00164